THE HOMESTEADER

It's damned hard work, homesteading. And when there are men who'll do anything to keep you from settling, it can be your last chance . . .

Jed Holley had staked a claim on Shavano Creek. There were only a few homesteaders there, but that was a few too many for men like the Custis brothers. And they were mean enough and tough enough to do something about it. Suddenly Jed was dead. So when Carl Holley came into town to track down his brother's killer the word spread like wildfire. Would they dare to kill him too?

THE HOMESTEADER

Lewis B. Patten

GUNSMOKE

This hardback edition 2003
by Chivers Press
by arrangement with
Golden West Literary Agency

ISBN 0 7540 8225 3

British Library Cataloguing in Publication Data available.

Printed and bound in Great Britain by
Antony Rowe Ltd, Chippenham, Wiltshire

CHAPTER 1

All day the stagecoach rattled over the rocky, winding road that bordered the bank-full Arkansas. Red dust rose in blinding clouds, sometimes drifting forward over the coach on the brisk wind that blew out of the south.

There were three passengers: a weathered, strong-faced woman of thirty-five, a middle-aged hardware salesman out of Denver a hundred and fifty miles to the east, and a muscular man who looked to be nearing thirty, plainly uncomfortable in a stand-up celluloid collar and rumpled black Sunday suit.

His face was roughened by sun and weather and said "farmer" plainly and unmistakably to anyone who looked. The woman had been studying him all day with eyes that never thawed from their first disapproving coldness, assumed when she discovered that their destinations were the same—Wild Horse on the Arkansas.

He had boarded the stage in Pueblo, having reached there by train. He sat silently on the right side of the coach, facing toward the front. His eyes stared out at the mountainous terrain, never losing interest despite the dust, the jolting of the coach and the discomfort of his suit.

Now, as the coach neared its destination, the woman across from him began to probe. "Are you staying in Wild Horse long, Mr. . . . ?"

He turned his eyes on her, steady, calm, blue-gray eyes that had the effect of making her flush with confusion. He

5

did not supply his name but said, "I don't know exactly," and let it go at that.

"Do you have property near Wild Horse?" she insisted stubbornly.

He let his eyes rest once more on her face. The glance was long and there was a faint frown on his forehead now. He saw the dull flush that mounted once more into her cheeks and looked quickly away, puzzled by her insistence but sorry he had embarrassed her. He said, "You might say that, I suppose."

They'd know soon enough in Wild Horse who he was and why he had come. But he hoped to find out some things before they learned his name.

The woman mustered a smile. "I'm Nell Kellison. My husband and I have a ranch on Shavano Creek."

He did not reply, nor did he look at her. She said, "I didn't catch your name."

"I didn't give it, ma'am."

There was a momentary silence. Then Nell Kellison said, "Well! I do declare! A body tries to be friendly and that's all the thanks they get!"

He glanced at her, his eyes sharper than before. "You weren't trying to be friendly, Mrs. Kellison. You were trying to find out who I am and what I'm doing here."

The blood drained out of her face. Her mouth thinned and her eyes hardened with anger.

The hardware salesman looked uneasily from one to the other, then stared out the window again. Mrs. Kellison followed suit for what seemed like a long time. At last, unable to maintain silence any longer, she turned her head. "An honest man wouldn't be so secretive," she said triumphantly.

That brought a smile to the man's wide mouth. It softened all the harsh lines of his face. He said softly, "And a dishonest man would be trying to appear honest, don't you think?"

She didn't answer that and it was plain that he had only further angered her. The stage rocked around a bend in the road and the town of Wild Horse became visible ahead.

Now the face of the man turned sombre, for this was the

place where his brother Jed had died. By gunshot, the letter had advised. So far as he knew, the killer had not been caught.

The business section of town lay on both sides of the main thoroughfare, which, according to a street sign, was named Shavano Street. There was a plank bridge short of the stage depot by about a block. It crossed Shavano Creek, at this time of year a roaring cataract that could be heard all over town.

The coach ground to a stop in front of a frame, false-fronted building bearing the sign "Arkansas and South Park Stageline." A man opened the door and helped Mrs. Kellison to the ground. The hardware salesman followed and the farmer stepped out last. He waited patiently until his carpetbag was handed down, then turned and headed for the hotel, half a block away. He drew a few curious stares from people along the street.

There were a couple of leather-covered settees and several chairs, similarly upholstered, in the hotel lobby. There were half a dozen brass spittoons. The man walked to the desk and put down his bag. A faint frown creased his forehead as the clerk shoved the register at him. He hesitated briefly, then wrote "Cole Holley" in a firm, decisive hand. He would have liked to keep his name to himself for a few hours but he didn't want to sign a false name to the hotel register.

Without looking at the name, the clerk said, "Number eight" and handed him a key.

Holley climbed the stairs. He found his room, unlocked the door and went inside. He dropped his bag on the bed, crossed to the window and briefly looked down into the street. An unfamiliar impatience kept tugging at him and at last he turned, crossed to the door, went out and locked it behind him. He descended the stairs to the lobby. The clerk was staring at him now. He had made the connection, thought Holley wryly to himself.

The sun was low in the sky behind the town. There were mountains to the west, high mountains still capped with snow. Between the town and the mountains was the valley of Shavano Creek, where Mrs. Kellison had said she and

7

her husband had their ranch. The valley of Shavano Creek was also where Jed's place was.

Holley turned toward a stone block building he had noticed coming into town. There was a green-painted bench in front, and the windows had bars on them. A sign over the door said "Sheriff."

He wasn't sure whether the sheriff would be in or not since it was suppertime, but he tried the door. It was unlocked so he went inside.

A gray-haired man looked up from a swivel chair. His skin was like leather and his eyes were blue. He wore a thick mustache, the ends of which were yellowed, either from chewing tobacco or cigars. Holley said, "I'm Cole Holley, Jed's brother. You wrote to me."

The swivel chair creaked as the sheriff got to his feet. He stuck out his hand and Holley took it, finding its grip neither too strong nor too weak. That impressed him favorably even if the whiskers on the sheriff's face and his dirty shirt did not. The sheriff said unnecessarily, "Burt Mexico, Mr. Holley. I'm the sheriff here."

Holley studied his face. He asked, "Have you caught Jed's killer yet?"

Mexico shook his head.

"Why not?"

The question was blunt and so was Holley's tone. The sheriff seemed disconcerted momentarily but at last he said, "Because I don't know who it was."

"Why was he killed? Was it robbery?"

Mexico shook his head.

Holley waited. The sheriff walked to the window and stared out into the street. "We've got a situation here that's probably different from anything back east. This country was settled back in '61 and '62. The people who settled it had to fight Indians and weather and a lot of other things. They started from scratch and some of them actually lived in caves and tents until they could get something better built. Those first settlers think they own the valley of Shavano Creek. Some ways I can't blame 'em for feeling the way they do. They made this country what it is. They built houses and roads and ditches so's they could irrigate.

8

They killed off the wolves and grizzly bears so their cattle would be safe. Now the government says any Johnny-come-lately can file on a hundred and sixty acres up there no matter who's claiming it."

"And my brother was one of the Johnny-come-latelies?"

Mexico nodded without turning his head.

"Which gave them a license to kill him. Is that what you're telling me?"

The sheriff turned. "I didn't say that and you know it."

"Then if you know why he was killed . . . if you know he was killed because he was stepping on the toes of the original settlers, why can't you find his murderer?"

"It's not as easy as you make it sound."

"If you can't find the killer, maybe I'd better see what I can do."

Mexico said, "Stay out of this, Mr. Holley, or I'll just have another killing on my hands. I'll eventually find out who the killer is. Just give me a little time."

"Where's his homestead? I want to see it."

"You figuring on claiming it?"

With deceptive mildness Holley said, "Maybe. If that's what it will take to smoke the killer out."

"You got a gun?"

Holley shook his head. "I'm a farmer, Mr. Mexico. Where I come from a man doesn't need a gun."

"I'd get one if I was you."

"Because you can't guarantee I won't get shot?"

The sheriff nodded. "This is one damn big county. I can't be everyplace."

"What if I get you a name? What if I find out who killed Jed?"

"You bring me a name and enough evidence to convict and I'll arrest the man quick enough. I'll see that he comes to trial. You may think I'm weaseling out of my responsibility or that I condone murder, but neither of those things is true. I just happen to know what I'm up against."

Holley said, "Give me directions for getting to his place. I want to look at it."

"That ain't hard. It's the sixth house after you leave

9

town on the Shavano Creek road. Ain't much. Just a one-room shack made out of slabs from the sawmill over on Trout Creek Pass."

Holley nodded. He went out into the street. He was hungry and tired from jolting back and forth in the coach all day. A feeling of irritability was stirring him. He walked down the street toward the livery stable looming up high against the flaming sky.

He had a farm back in Illinois with which he was perfectly satisfied. It had a comfortable house on it and he certainly didn't need a homestead claim on which there was a one-room shack made out of slabs from the sawmill up on Trout Creek Pass.

But he didn't intend to tell anybody he wasn't interested in Jed's place. He wanted everyone to think he meant to take up where Jed left off. If they had killed Jed for settling in the valley of Shavano Creek, then they'd have the same motive for killing his brother Cole.

He put the carpetbag down on the ground outside the stable door and stepped inside. If he hurried, he could drive out to Jed's place on Shavano Creek before it turned completely dark.

CHAPTER 2

His eye caught movement on his right, and close, but no warning stirred in him. Only when something slammed against the side of his head with force like a sledge, did he know he had walked into the same kind of trouble that had resulted, for Jed, in death. They had learned his name from the clerk at the hotel. They knew why he was here. They

10

had no intention of permitting him to stay.

Groggy, he staggered to one side, trying to penetrate the dimness inside the stable with his glance. He could see shapes and forms, but the faces were blurred by oncoming darkness. And besides, things were happening much too fast for noticing faces and remembering even if the light had been strong enough. These men were grimly efficient and determined. How many of them were here, he had no way of knowing. But he knew one thing. He could die here. He could die right here on this dirty floor.

Another fist slammed into the other side of his head, nearly tearing loose his ear. He could feel the warmth of blood running down the side of his face. He tried to back into the stronger light outside, but someone yelled hoarsely, "Don't let the bastard get away!"

A body slammed against him, carrying him past the doorway and back into the shadows beyond. He rolled on the floor, which had a covering of straw and dry manure. Before he could recover himself and rise, half a dozen boots kicked out at him, some missing, some connecting. One caught him in the ribs with pain so excruciating he gasped with it. Another caught him in the leg, numbing it. A third slammed into his head, making his ears ring, making bright lights dance before his eyes.

The instinct for self-preservation was strong. He rolled away, trying to cover his belly with his arms. Something else was also stirring in him now, an emotion as strong as that of self-preservation. It was outrage. It was fury that they would attack him like this, men who did not even know him except by name.

He fought to his knees, then to his feet, borne back by the weight of their numbers as he did. He slammed against the wall of the stable tackroom. A nail sticking out of the wall, placed there to hang something from, gouged him cruelly in the back. It felt as if the nail, head and all, had gone into his body a couple of inches but he supposed it only felt that way. A bony fist slammed into his mouth, and another into his belly, making him double forward in spite of himself.

So far he hadn't struck a blow and this fact angered him

11

almost as much as the unprovoked attack. But he also knew his fists weren't going to stop these men. What punishment his fists could inflict on them would be so slight compared to the way they were punishing him that it wouldn't even count.

If he was going to survive he had better find a weapon—soon. And to find a weapon, he had to get away from them, if only temporarily.

He whirled and plunged away along the wall. He slammed into a man's body. He sent the man sprawling, and tripped over his body, and fell headlong himself. But he didn't remain motionless. He clawed on, crawling, coming to his feet as soon as he could and plunging on to the deeper shadows farther into the stable's interior. They came running after him, panting from the exertion and excitement of beating him, but not calling to each other, nor crying out any names that he might later recognize.

He crashed into the chest-high wall of a stall, and felt a bridle hanging from it. He kept on, but stumbled and fell over something lying on the floor.

They were on him like a pack of wolves. He was strong and solid but there is a limit to what even a solid and muscular man can absorb. Their kicks rained on him. Someone had a club of some kind or another, an axe handle or plank, and it crashed down across his back, driving his face into the dusty manure on the floor. A voice yelled, "Don't kill him. Don't kill him, damn it, or we'll have Mexico after us for it."

Holley kept fighting, not that he now felt much hope of escape. He got away again, and made it to his feet, and plunged down a long, darkened alleyway toward the rear door leading to the corrals out back. The door made a square of light, and suddenly in that dim light Holley saw it—a pitchfork leaning against the wall of one of the stalls.

They were close behind him now, but he lunged for the pitchfork, seized it and came whirling around, fighting for balance, angry enough to kill.

A man plunged into range and he jabbed viciously. The fork sank a single tine into the man's thigh and he let out a high yell of surprise and pain.

12

Holley yanked the fork free before the man could fall. He backed away. If he let them come in close they'd overwhelm him and even though he managed to jab one or two of them with the fork, it wouldn't help him in the end.

The man he had jabbed in the thigh was whimpering, and another man somewhere there in the shadows said savagely, "Get out of the way, God damn it. I'll fix the son-of-a-bitch for good!"

"Don't shoot him! Don't shoot unless you want Mexico down here."

"To hell with Mexico!"

Some part of Holley's memory might later recall the voices that were speaking now. Perhaps he would recognize them, perhaps he would not. They were enraged and changed by passion from their normal quality.

But he understood two things. They would be satisfied with nothing less than beating him into unconsciousness. Nor could he defeat them, not by himself, not even with the help of the pitchfork. Most or all of them had guns. If he carried the attack to them, they would simply shoot him down, and scatter before the sheriff could arrive.

He knew what he ought to do. He should drop the fork and try to escape, knowing all the time that it was impossible. He should let them catch him, let them beat him into unconsciousness. That would satisfy them and they would leave.

Yet even knowing that this was the smart thing to do, he also knew he could never do it. Not if it cost him his life. He was angry; he was hurt and he didn't even know who his assailants were. Nor did they know him. Except by name. They only knew he was Jed Holley's brother and claimant to his homestead on Shavano Creek.

There had to be another way. And suddenly he knew what it was. He would force them to shoot. Gunshots would bring the sheriff and the men would scatter and disappear.

He raised the pitchfork and held it like a spear. He no longer cared whether he killed one of them or not. He took aim and threw the fork and he saw it catch one of the men advancing toward him in the belly. The man squawled like

13

a stuck hog and fell, writhing, to the floor.

Holley didn't wait. He turned and ducked behind the chest-high frame wall of the stall. Bent low, he ran, and he heard someone bawl, "He got Sam! Kill the bastard! Now!"

A gunshot rang out, and a moment later, another. Good, he thought. Now the sheriff will be coming here.

Running, he stumbled over some irregularity in the floor and fell.

More gunshots rang out, the bullets thudding into the wall beyond him and above his head. He rolled up close against the partition of one of the stalls, the reek of manure strong in his nostrils. A horse was plunging in a stall somewhere, terrified and trying to escape. Men were milling around, searching blindly for him. . . .

One ran past only a couple of feet away. Holley tried to make his breathing slow and regular despite the laboring of his lungs.

There was a warm spot on his back where the nail had penetrated. There was another warm spot on his neck where blood from his torn ear trickled down. His nose was smashed and so was his mouth. One of his eyes burned and felt puffy and he knew it would be black, perhaps even swelled shut tomorrow. They had marked him up good, damn them, but he had inflicted his share of punishment as well. One of them had a wound in the leg from the rusty, filthy pitchfork and another had a wound in the abdomen. These two, at least, would be identifiable tomorrow. These two would give him a place to start in his search for the man or men who had murdered Jed.

From the street door of the livery barn a harsh voice yelled, "What the hell's going on in here?"

Holley could hear his assailants leaving now, swiftly and stealthily by the rear door. Their forms were briefly visible against the square of gray light framed by the opening. And suddenly it was quiet inside the stable, except for the horse plunging in his stall, except for Holley's labored breathing and except for the sound of the sheriff's footsteps advancing toward him.

14

Holley called, "It's Cole Holley, Sheriff. I'm coming out."

He got to his feet and staggered toward the front of the livery barn. Mexico shouted, "Anybody else in here?"

No one answered him. Holley supposed the two men he had stabbed with the pitchfork had been carried off by their friends. He reached the sheriff and stood there, panting heavily, hurting all over now. He said, "I came down here to hire a rig and they jumped me when I came in the door."

"Who jumped you?"

Holley shrugged, and winced with the pain the movement caused. He said, "You'll know two of them tomorrow. One has a pitchfork wound in the leg and the other got a tine in the belly."

The sheriff sighed. "All right, come on. I'll take you over to see the doc. How bad are you hurt?"

"I got a rusty nail jabbed into my back. Otherwise nothing that won't heal all right in a week or so."

"I hope you think that stinking piece of land is worth all this."

"I'm not doing this over a piece of land."

"No, I suppose you're not." The sheriff led the way out into the street. The flaming clouds had faded now and the sky was a uniform, dingy gray. Holley couldn't see anybody in the street, but two or three stores had lamps burning inside, illuminating their windows and sometimes a square of boardwalk immediately in front of their open doors.

Seeing Jed's place would have to wait until tomorrow, he thought. But seeing it didn't really matter anymore. He had succeeded in stirring up the hornet's nest, which was what he had come here to do.

He followed the sheriff along the street, limping painfully. There was a two-story building next to the hotel. It had an outside stairway and the sheriff directed Holley up the stairs. A lamp burned in the office at the head of it and on the door the doctor's name was painted in black letters two inches high. The name was Hiram Rounds, and

15

after it were the letters M.D.

The doctor glanced up from his desk as they came in. He looked at Holley, then glanced questioningly at Mexico. The sheriff said, "He was beat up down at the stable, Doc. Fix him up."

Dr. Rounds got up. He beckoned Holley to a chair. Painfully Holley began to remove his coat and shirt, both of which were torn and covered with manure.

The sheriff said, "There are going to be two pitchfork wounds for you to treat somewhere in town tonight. I'll be coming to you for the men's names tomorrow."

The doctor didn't answer him. He was looking at the wound on Holley's back, the one made by the nail. "Got this from a rusty nail, I suppose."

"Uh huh. I got slammed against a wall."

The doctor's voice was angry and irritable. "I don't know why the hell people can't find a cleaner place to fight. You've got this, and two other men have pitchfork wounds. If all three of you don't get blood poisoning it will be a miracle."

Holley didn't make a reply because he knew the doctor expected none. Hiram Rounds got a pan full of water and dumped some kind of strong disinfectant into it. He got some clean cloths and began to wash the abrasions on Holley's face and back. He grumbled angrily all the time he was doing it, but his hands were gentler than his tongue. Even so, Holley's face turned white with pain half a dozen times.

The sheriff stayed, lounging in the doorway, watching. When the doctor had finished taking three stitches in Holley's torn ear and when he had begun to bandage him, the sheriff asked, "What now, Mr. Holley? Are you going to be sensible and let me handle your brother's murder the way I'm supposed to do? Or are you going to go on trying to handle it yourself?"

Holley glanced at him. He asked, "Was Jed the only homesteader on Shavano Creek?"

Burt Mexico shook his head.

"But he was the first one killed?"

"What do you mean, the first one?" Mexico asked

16

plaintively. "What makes you think that others might get killed?"

"How many other homesteaders are there on Shavano Creek?"

"Two families."

"Are they making plans to move on out?"

"One of them is."

"And the other one?"

"I guess they're going to stay."

"Any new people planning to homestead on Shavano Creek?"

The sheriff shook his head.

"Then those people up there made their point when they killed my brother, didn't they? Provided they can get me to leave, and provided they can persuade that last homesteading family to leave."

"I guess you might say that. People around here kind of feel like these ranchers up there are entitled to that land."

"I wonder if a federal judge would think they were."

The sheriff stared at him uneasily. Then, without another word, he turned and went out the door. Holley heard him clumping heavily down the stairs.

CHAPTER 3

When the doctor had finished with him, Holley got up, found his shirt and shrugged carefully into it. He put on his coat but he did not replace either his collar or his tie. He stuffed them into the pocket of the coat.

From his pants pocket he took out a cavernous coin purse and dumped some of the coins into his hand. "How much for the patch job, Doc?"

"Fifty cents all right?"

Holley handed him a half dollar and replaced the rest in the coin purse which he then returned to his pocket.

The doctor was studying him. "You'd better come back in a day or two and let me look at that puncture wound on your back. Particularly if it should get red or unusually sore."

"All right."

"Just as a matter of curiosity, Mr. Holley, how many of them were there down at the stable a while ago?"

"Six or eight, I suppose."

"And you held them off by yourself, without a gun?"

"I found that pitchfork. Right afterward the sheriff interrupted and stopped the fight."

The doctor was shaking his head. "You may not be so lucky next time."

Holley felt a stir of irritability. "I suppose you agree with the sheriff. I suppose you think I ought to go back where I came from and forget what happened to my brother Jed."

"Nothing you do will bring him back. But don't sell Burt Mexico short, Mr. Holley. He's a good man and an honest sheriff. He'll find the man who killed your brother if anybody can."

Holley said sourly, "I think I can do it quicker. That way I'll be sure that it gets done."

Dr. Rounds dumped some water into a pan and began to wash his hands. He was short and stocky and was probably fifty-five years old. He was almost completely bald and wore a mustache, clipped short and graying like what remained of his hair. He had a sagging paunch and there were pouches underneath his eyes, which gave him a sad expression. His clothes were wrinkled and there was a gravy spot on his shirt front. Holley guessed he was probably a bachelor who lived alone.

Rounds turned to face him again, drying his hands. "I expect I'll be seeing you again, Mr. Holley, if you stick to your determination to stir up that hornet's nest on Shavano Creek."

18

Holley grinned. He liked the doctor but he couldn't fail to feel the doctor's obvious disapproval of his presence here. He said, "Maybe you ought to give me a special rate."

Rounds didn't smile. "I just hope it's me that gets you next time and not the undertaker."

There didn't seem to be anything to say after that. Holley thanked him again, then went out the door. He stood for a moment on the landing, staring down into the street.

The sky had cleared and was dotted now with stars. There was a breeze blowing out of the west, cool from the snows it had crossed, but carrying the indefinable smell of spring, of things growing and pushing through the awakening soil.

Holley went heavily down the stairs. He felt depressed. Even if he did find Jed's killer, he doubted if it would relieve the way he felt because he knew he was partially responsible for Jed's death.

He stared toward the stable looming against the sky farther down the street. The doctor was right. He would have more trouble with the ranchers on Shavano Creek. They thought they were in the right and apparently thought that whatever they had to do to hold their land was justified. It was doubtful if he or anyone else was going to convince them otherwise.

Yet he knew he could not give up. He owed it to Jed to see that his killer paid the penalty. Maybe he owed it to that other homesteading family to side with them. Mostly, he guessed, he owed it to himself to do what he believed was right.

He walked toward the hotel, stiff and sore from the beating he had taken, filthy and smelly from rolling in the manure on the stable floor. He needed a bath and meant to get one as soon as he reached the hotel.

His mind kept returning to his brother Jed. Maybe, he thought, if he'd given Jed more to say about running the farm in Illinois he wouldn't have come out here to homestead and if he hadn't done that, he wouldn't have

19

been killed. He shook his head, knowing he shouldn't blame himself. Jed had just grown up. He had left home because he wanted to.

He reached the hotel and went inside. He crossed to the desk and spoke to the clerk. "I'd like some hot water sent up to my room. I want to take a bath."

The clerk stared at him with startled eyes. "What happened!"

"Some men jumped me down at the livery barn."

"Did they get anything?"

"I don't think it was a robbery attempt."

"What was it, then?" The clerk sounded scared.

"I don't think they want me nosing into my brother's death. You gave them my name, didn't you?"

The clerk's face suddenly turned hot. "I . . . I didn't know they . . ."

"You didn't know they'd try to kill me? Is that what you were going to say?"

The clerk's face had lost all its color now. It seemed almost gray. Holley asked, "Who did you give my name to?"

The clerk's voice was scarcely audible. "To Ben Custis is all."

Holley nodded, and turned to go. The clerk asked desperately, "You won't tell him I told you, will you?"

"Is there any reason why I shouldn't?"

The clerk shook his head miserably. Holley turned, crossed to the stairs and climbed them wearily. He supposed he'd feel better after he'd bathed and had something to eat, but right now he just felt mean and irritable. He wished someone would pick a fight with him.

He had to wait about fifteen minutes before the water came. It was brought by an elderly man, in two heavy buckets. One was filled with hot water, the other with cold.

Holley dumped the hot water into the tub, then added the cold slowly until the temperature suited him. He took off his clothes. He rummaged through his coat until he found a cigar that was not too badly broken to smoke. He lighted it, got into the tub, leaned back and closed his eyes. He puffed on the cigar luxuriously.

He thought of the family of homesteaders on Shavano Creek. It took a special kind of courage to stay up there with every hand against them, with all the other homesteaders gone. He was suddenly anxious to see them and talk to them. He wanted to know what kind of people they really were.

Because he hadn't been expecting it, the knock on his door startled him. He opened his eyes, hesitated a moment, then called, "Come in."

The door opened. A man stood framed in it, a thick, heavyset, ugly man, perhaps fifty or fifty-five years old, with a close-cropped shock of gray-white hair and skin like mahogany. He wore a wide-brimmed Texas hat and high-heeled Texas boots with spurs on them. There was a sagging belt around his waist, filled with cartridges, that supported a holstered revolver with worn walnut grips. His voice was thick and harsh. "I guess you're Cole Holley. Right?"

Holley nodded. He said irritably, "If you're coming in, do it and close the door. There's a draft."

The man came in and pushed the door closed behind him. He was scowling at Holley's tone and he stared down at Holley with no apparent embarrassment. Holley weighed a hundred and ninety pounds, all of it hard muscle and bone. His face and neck and hands were dark from the sun but the rest of his body was white. The stranger said, "My name's Custis. Ben Custis. You put up a pretty good fight over at the livery barn a while ago."

"How do you know that?"

"I was there. I came to tell you that if you're not on the stage tomorrow, we'll work on you again. Only we won't use kid gloves on you next time. We'll . . ."

"Kill me like you did my brother Jed?"

Custis stared coldly at him.

Holley picked up the bar of soap from the dish beside the tub and began to lather one of his legs. Custis asked, in a more reasonable tone, "Want to sell your brother's homestead claim?"

"I haven't heard an offer yet."

"And you may not. But if you want to sell, I'll see what the rest of the boys will do."

Holley said, "The price went up considerably over at the stable a while ago."

Custis was scowling again. His eyes were cold and angry. "You've got until noon tomorrow to make up your mind."

Holley's own temper was stirring now. "What if I was to tell you to go to hell?"

Custis shrugged.

For several moments neither spoke. Then, in an almost pleading tone, Custis said, "There's a lot more involved in this than one homestead claim. If you and the Nordlanders manage to hang on, it's going to bring a whole damn mob of other homesteaders that want a piece of land on Shavano Creek. First thing you know, those of us who settled it originally won't have anything."

"You can homestead like anybody else."

"And what good will a hundred and sixty acres apiece do us?"

"It was enough for my brother Jed. It's apparently enough for the Nordlander family."

"Well, it ain't enough for us. We got cattle, mister. We run 'em out in the mountains in the summertime and we bring 'em down into the valley and feed 'em hay in the wintertime. A man would starve to death trying to feed cattle with the hay he could raise on a hundred and sixty acre homestead claim."

"It's a law, Mr. Custis. It's a federal law and this is a federal territory."

"Then you're not going to leave?"

"No. And you can tell your friends that I'm going to swear out two criminal assault complaints just as soon as I learn the names of the men with the pitchfork wounds."

Custis nodded coldly, "Suit yourself. Just . . ." Apparently deciding any more threats would be a waste of breath, he backed out the door and pulled it closed.

Holley finished his bath, got out and dried himself. Frowning to himself, he dressed in clean clothes that he took from his carpetbag. He brushed off his coat as best he could and put it on.

Custis had made one thing very clear. The ranchers on Shavano Creek would beat him again if they got the chance. They'd kill him the way they had killed Jed if they got an opportunity. It was open season on him from this moment on.

He couldn't help the coldness that settled in his chest. He couldn't help the uneasiness that crept through his mind. He went out and descended the stairs to the lobby. They might have him scared but they had no way of knowing it. He certainly wasn't going to let it show.

CHAPTER 4

There was a restaurant half a block down the street from the hotel. Holley went in and sat down at one of the tables near the door.

Two men at another table looked at him, scowled and looked away. He saw Nell Kellison with a dark-faced, middle-aged man and two children, a boy and girl he guessed must be twelve or thirteen years old. Mrs. Kellison did not acknowledge his nod, for which he couldn't blame her, he supposed. He hadn't been particularly courteous to her on the stagecoach earlier.

The waitress, a plain, colorless woman, brought a menu and he ordered roast beef. She hurried away with a furtive glance at the Kellisons.

When she returned, he waited until she had placed his dinner in front of him and then he asked, "Do you know the Nordlander family?"

She shot a quick glance at the Kellisons. He said wryly, "I doubt if they'll do anything to you for just answering a question. It isn't as though I was asking you to take sides."

She flushed painfully and then her eyes sparkled with anger. She said in a thin, clipped voice, "I know them.

23

Their place is at the mouth of Brush Creek."

"That empties into Shavano Creek, I suppose."

"Yes. About six or seven miles from town."

"Thank you."

She ducked her head by way of acknowledgment and hurried toward the kitchen. Holley ate quickly, not surprised that he failed completely to enjoy his food. Jed couldn't have been very happy here, he thought. Jed couldn't have liked being treated with hostility and suspicion any better than anybody else.

He was glad to finish his dinner, glad to be able to leave the restaurant. He put a quarter on the table to pay for it and went outside. He stood on the boardwalk long enough to light another cigar, which was somewhat the worse for wear. Then he walked toward the hotel.

At the desk, he bought a handful of cigars. There was no one in the lobby except the clerk, who treated him with reserved neutrality. As Holley turned away from the desk, the clerk asked timidly, "Did you tell him that I . . . ?"

Holley shook his head.

"Thank you, Mr. Holley. I appreciate . . ."

Holley swung back toward the desk. "Is everybody in town afraid of him?"

The clerk glanced around furtively. "Not just him, Mr. Holley. All of them. It's like some different kind of world up there on Shavano Creek. Several years ago they hanged three rustlers and didn't even tell the sheriff until it was all over with. Your brother . . ." He stopped suddenly and licked his lips.

"What about my brother?"

"Nothing, Mr. Holley. Nothing. I don't know a thing."

Holley studied him. The man was thoroughly frightened and it wasn't likely that he'd get much more out of him tonight. Besides, he was tired, and sore from the beating in the livery barn. He nodded and turned toward the stairs.

In his room, he locked the door and took off his pants and shirt. In his underwear, he lay down on the bed.

The sky was light when he awoke, but the sun was not yet up. He couldn't help groaning when he moved. Every muscle in his body was painfully sore. He licked his lips

24

and found them puffy and covered with dried blood. Painfully he got out of bed and crossed the room to stare into the cracked mirror on the wall.

One eye was blackened. There were several scabbed abrasions on his face. The bandage the doctor had stuck onto his ear with court plaster had come off during the night and the stitches were visible. He grinned ruefully at himself in the mirror, wincing with the pain the grin brought on.

Turning away, he dressed quickly. He put his things into the carpetbag, washed his face, then descended to the lobby. He put the key down on the desk.

A different clerk was on today, an older man. Holley paid for his room and went outside.

The sun was just coming over the mountain ridge east of the Arkansas. Holley walked to the livery stable and went inside.

There was a stableman present this morning. His expression said that he knew who Holley was and that he also knew what had happened here last night. Holley asked, "Where were you last night?"

"At supper." The man wouldn't meet his eyes. It was a reasonable answer, yet Holley had the feeling the stableman had been sent home by the ranchers to get him out of the way. They had probably guessed that he would be going out to see his brother's place on Shavano Creek yesterday while it still was light, and they had therefore set up their ambush at the livery barn.

Holley said, "I want a buggy. I may not bring it back for a day or two."

The man grumbled something, but he got a horse out of one of the stalls, harnessed him and led him back to where several buggies were. He backed the horse between the shafts and hooked him up. He drove the buggy to where Holley was waiting. "It'll be four bits a day."

"All right." Holley climbed into the buggy and drove out into the street. He took the Shavano Creek road leading out of town.

He didn't know exactly what he had expected to see on Shavano Creek. He certainly hadn't expected it to be as

25

beautiful as it was. In the distance to the west the high, snow-capped peaks of the Continental Divide made a jagged line against the flawless sky, turned pink by the rising sun. The peaks were probably fifteen or twenty miles away but they looked to be much closer than that.

The valley itself stretched away in great, undulating loops, in some places less than a half mile wide, in others wider than a mile.

On both sides were low brush- and cedar-covered hills. Farther up, spruce and quaking aspen grew, the spruce a dark, brooding green, the aspens lighter, their leaves shimmering in the sun.

The valley floor itself was one great hay meadow, stretching from side to side. Hay was already greening it, and in places Holley could see water spilling across from the irrigation ditches that separated the valley floor from the rougher land on both sides.

In the middle of the valley Shavano Creek tumbled, or sometimes ran deep and swift, or sometimes looped back and forth like a giant snake.

Holley drove the buggy horse at a steady trot. He counted the houses that he passed.

Most of them were built of logs, hand-hewn and chinked with clay. Some of the ranches had huge barns. In almost all of the hayfields a few brown haystacks sat, a residue of unused hay from the year before. Grazing cattle were everywhere.

Holley encountered no one on the road. He reached his brother's house and drove down the lane to it. He halted the horse, climbed out and snapped the weight to the horse's bridle to hold him still.

He looked at the shack, at the lean-to on one side of it, a lean-to which had obviously served as a stable for Jed's saddle horse. He turned from the shack and stared around at what he judged to be Jed's homestead claim.

It was fenced with barbed wire, but with only two wires. Apparently Jed hadn't been able to afford more than two or else he just hadn't gotten around to stringing it. Two wires would keep horses out, thought Holley, but they wouldn't even slow cattle down.

26

From here, it looked as though less than a fourth of Jed's hundred and sixty acres were below the ditch. Holley shook his head. Men died for a variety of things. In itself, this homestead claim certainly wasn't worth dying for. But Jed's right to exist . . . his right to homestead according to the law . . . his equality as a man . . . these things were worth whatever they might cost. In Jed's case, the price had been his life. Holley wondered briefly if Jed had known when he started what the price might be.

He returned to the buggy and got his carpetbag. He carried it inside the house.

The inside was no better than the outside. It was untidy. The table was covered with dirty dishes. The packed dirt floor was unswept. The bunk was unmade.

Holley swept the place out first. Then he made the bed. Then he got water from the creek and built a fire in the sheet-iron stove. When the water was hot, he washed the dishes and wiped the table off. Finished with that, he went out and climbed into the buggy. He drove back to the road and west along it toward the mouth of a valley that joined this one a couple of miles farther on. He wanted to see the Nordlanders. He wanted to talk to them. He wanted to know if he was going to have to fight this fight alone, or if he would have help.

It wasn't hard to tell that the Nordlanders were homesteaders. Their house had not the solid look that characterized the homes of the ranchers that had originally settled here. Like Jed's shack, it was covered with slabs on the outside. The roof was also covered with slabs, lapped over so that they would shed water.

The Nordlanders had a barn of sorts. It was almost as big as the house and similarly constructed. There were a few white chickens scratching in the yard. There were a couple of milch cows in the corral. And there was a woman in the yard, hanging a washing on the line.

Holley pulled the buggy to a halt. He climbed out and attached the weight to the bridle. He approached the woman, removing his hat as he did. She watched his approach warily.

She was a young woman, in her middle twenties, he

27

thought. She seemed rather small, but judging from the size of the laundry basket she had carried out, she wasn't weak. Her hair was dark, her face tanned. Her eyes were blue. Unsmilingly she looked at him.

Holley said, "You must be Mrs. Nordlander."

She nodded. "Yes."

"I'm Cole Holley, Jed Holley's brother."

Her demeanor changed instantly. She came toward him, wiping her hands on her apron. She extended her hand and he took it, finding it damp but strong and firm.

He studied her face. It was a face of singular strength, but oddly enough the strength in no way detracted from its beauty. Her mouth was full, her chin strong. Her cheekbones were high and her cheeks somewhat hollow beneath them. He held her hand longer than he intended, and saw a slight flush mount into her face.

Suddenly and unaccountably embarrassed himself, he released her hand. She said quickly, "I'm so sorry about Jed, Mr. Holley."

"Thank you."

"Are you going to finish proving up on his homestead claim?"

He nodded. Either that, or refile on it in my own name. Whatever the law requires me to do."

"They won't let you stay, Mr. Holley. They'll try driving you away just like they've tried driving the rest of us away."

Her voice had an arresting quality. He liked listening to her speak. He looked beyond her toward the house and saw the faces of two small children peering at him from the door. He asked, "Where is your husband, Mrs. Nordlander?" and suddenly realized that he had brought her husband into the conversation deliberately.

She turned her head to look toward the west. Following her glance, Holley saw a man in overalls walking toward them. The man was still nearly a quarter mile away, but even at this distance Holley could tell that he was elderly.

The man was frowning as he came into the yard. He carried a shovel as if it was a weapon. He was, indeed, much older than his wife. Holley judged he was in his early

28

seventies. Mrs. Nordlander said almost breathlessly, "Lars, this is Mr. Holley. He is Jed's brother from the east."

Nordlander's face relaxed immediately the way his wife's had done. The children had come from the house. They approached and stood beside Nordlander, each of them taking one of his calloused hands. Nordlander might be old enough to be his wife's grandfather, but there was no doubt about what the children thought of him.

Nordlander said in a heavy Scandinavian accent, "Well, come in, come in. We will have some coffee or something while we talk."

His wife took the children's hands and walked toward the house. Holley followed, with Nordlander at his side.

When they reached the house, Nordlander held the door for him. Holley stepped inside. Mrs. Nordlander had turned and was looking at his bruised and battered face. Lars Nordlander, coming in behind him, said, "It looks as if they have already found you, Mr. Holley, and tried to discourage you."

Holley nodded.

"And did they discourage you?"

Holley grinned. "I'm still here, so I guess not."

"Do you want a little advice from an old man, Mr. Holley?"

Holley nodded, sobering.

"Let them have that homestead claim. Let it go back to the government. It is not worth dying for."

"What about your claim, Mr. Nordlander? Is it worth dying for?"

Nordlander smiled. "I am an old man. I have not as much to lose as you."

Holley glanced at Mrs. Nordlander and then at the two children at her side. "I'd say you had much more."

She flushed with pleasure at the compliment. Nordlander stared at Holley as though trying to evaluate him. He said, "The coffee, Gerda. Will you get the coffee please?"

She turned and went toward the stove. Nordlander said, "Sit down, Mr. Holley, and tell me what happened to you in town."

CHAPTER 5

Holley drank his coffee, accepted a second cup and drank that too. The children, a girl of five and a boy about a year younger, stared at him unblinkingly all the time. They made him uncomfortable because he wasn't used to children, but he knew they weren't being intentionally rude. They were simply curious. Twice Mrs. Nordlander noticed their steady scrutiny without scolding them. She only smiled at Holley, as though she expected him to understand.

Both Lars Nordlander and his wife came out into the yard with him when he left, and now their steady glances were as unnerving as those of the children had been earlier. It was as though they were still trying to evaluate him, trying to decide whether he would stand against the ranchers when the pressure was increased.

He climbed into the buggy. They stood on the ground looking up at him. Nordlander said, "I am being selfish when I say I am glad you have come and glad you are going to stay. They will try to drive you out before they turn to us, but we will help you because your fight is our fight too. You are welcome here at any time."

Holley smiled. "Thanks." He drove out of the yard. At the main road he turned his head. Nordlander was trudging away in the direction from which he had come earlier. The children had returned to their play. Gerda Nordlander was the only one looking after him. Her hand was raised to shield her eyes from the glare of the sun. The breeze stirred her hair and skirt. She made a straight and lovely figure there and he knew he would remember her.

He turned toward Jed's place, trying to put Gerda Nordlander out of his thoughts. There was a plume of smoke ahead, and he wondered what could be burning at this time of year.

He had driven nearly halfway before he realized the smoke was coming from the shack Jed had built on his homestead claim. When he did realize it, he whipped the buggy horse to a gallop.

The buggy rocked back and forth on the rough, uneven road. Holley knew he was going to be too late. By the time he arrived the cabin would be no more than a pile of smoldering ashes on the ground. And even if it was not yet completely destroyed, there would be little he could do. There would be nothing in which he could carry water to fight the blaze. All buckets and utensils were inside the shack.

The violent motion of the buggy made all the aches in his body begin to hurt again and a certain bleakness came into his thoughts. How could he fight the entrenched cattlemen in this valley by himself? They would stop at nothing to get rid of him. Murder, assault, arson—they had already committed all of these crimes. What chance did he have to fight them successfully?

The sheriff had been right about one thing. He had to have a gun. Words weren't going to sway them and fists, he had discovered, were inadequate. If he was going to survive, he would have to fight them on their own terms, with their own weapons.

The cabin was, indeed, only a pile of embers when he arrived. The horse balked at going close, so he stopped the buggy well clear of the smoldering rubble and on the windward side. He got down and clipped the weight to the bridle.

Slowly he walked toward what was left of the shack. And suddenly he knew what he was going to do. There would be tracks here of the man or men who had fired it. He wasn't an expert tracker, but even an Illinois farm boy receives some experience in following the trails of animals.

Before doing anything, Holley stared around at the

31

landscape, taking his time, letting no possible place of concealment escape his scrutiny. Satisfied that he was not being observed, he began a circle of the remains of the cabin.

The tracks of Texas boots were difficult to miss because of the small heelprint, which stood out plainly among the tracks of Holley's shoes.

Widening his circle, Holley came upon horse tracks, and some droppings where two horses had been tied. Here he also found the boot tracks again.

He set out following the tracks. They headed straight across the hayfield and were easy to follow because the ground was soft. When he reached the fence, Holley found the wire cut. And now the trail of the two horses climbed through the scrub sagebrush toward the west.

It was slower going because the ground up here was dry. Several times Holley stopped and studied the land around him. He knew he might be walking into a planned ambush. He knew the cabin might have been burned in a deliberate attempt to make him retaliate.

The sun continued to climb toward its zenith in the sky, and then began its inexorable descent toward the snow-capped peaks of the Continental Divide. In mid-afternoon, Holley was still no more than three or four miles from his starting point. But he was taking his time, traveling slowly and carefully. He was almost sure that he had not been seen.

At sundown, he reached a spot less than a quarter mile from one of the valley ranches. Bellied down in the sagebrush, he stared at it.

The tracks led straight toward it. He saw a woman cross the yard to the henhouse, a lard pail in her hand. She returned to the house ten or fifteen minutes later. Holley supposed the pail was filled with eggs.

There was a comfortable two-story house down there, built of hand-hewn logs. The roof was thatched with split cedar shakes. There was a porch, on which some kind of vines grew, and there was a freshly plowed and planted vegetable garden out in back.

Besides the house, there was a chicken house, a towering

32

log barn, and a half a dozen smaller buildings that Holley couldn't identify. A few white chickens that had not yet gone to roost scratched aimlessly in the yard. A boy came from the brushy creek bottom driving two milch cows ahead of him.

It was a peaceful scene, not much different from the one he had observed driving into the Nordlanders place earlier. Yet down there were two who had deliberately set fire to his cabin. They might have been among those who attacked him in the livery barn last night. They might be the ones who had killed his brother Jed.

The boy drove the cows into the barn and went to the house for milk buckets. Not long afterward, he drove the cows out of the barn again and carried the filled buckets to the house.

It was getting dark. Holley could scarcely see the boy's figure in the yard. A square of light appeared where the house loomed against the sky, and another, and another, and another still. Smoke thickened at the chimney.

Holley was hungry, but he knew he couldn't eat yet for a while. He figured the ranch family was sitting at the supper table now. He got stiffly to his feet.

Careful to make no more noise than necessary, he approached the cluster of buildings. They undoubtedly had a dog, he thought, even though he hadn't seen one yet. The dog would bark.

He wasn't proud of what he was doing. He felt like a thief. But he also knew he had no choice. He had no other cheek to turn. He had to fight back now in a way these cattlemen would understand. He had to let them know that he could, and would, hurt them every time they hurt him.

They had attacked him in town last night without provocation. They had burned his shack today in another attempt to make him leave. They had killed Jed and they would kill him if they could. And once he was gone, they would start on the Nordlanders.

He went forward stealthily. He approached the buildings from the creek bottom, executing a wide circle to make this possible. He reached the rear of the barn in complete darkness.

A slight breeze blew toward him from the house, bringing the smell of frying meat. His mouth watered and he thought his stomach was going to cramp, but it did not. At least, he thought, the breeze was in his favor. If they had dogs, the dogs would not be able to catch his scent.

There was no door at the rear of the barn, but there was a window. It was open, so he pulled himself up and eased through the opening.

A horse saw him and shifted in his stall nervously. Holley dropped to the floor and waited for a moment, blind in the complete darkness here. He could smell the hay in the loft. There also was the smell of horses and harness leather and the smell of manure.

He could now see the square of gray that marked the open doors at the other end of the barn. Between the doors and where he stood he saw a ladder leading to the loft.

Testing each step, he moved toward it. He reached it without incident and climbed quickly up. Most of the hay was gone, used up during the past winter, but there was a pile of loose grass hay against the wall. He judged there was at least a ton. Dry as it was, once he lighted it, it would be inextinguishable.

He fumbled in his pocket for a match. Lighting it against the ladder, he tossed it into the pile of hay.

He had to wait only an instant because the flame spread through it almost explosively. Dropping to the floor of the barn, he ran now toward the window at its end. Climbing up, he dropped through.

A dog rushed into the barn, barking furiously. Holley ran down into the creek bottom, plunged recklessly through the underbrush and came out on the other side. He climbed the hillside at a steady trot. He knew they couldn't catch him now. He also knew they wouldn't try. But they would trail him tomorrow as soon as it was light. If they didn't already know who had set the fire, they would find out tomorrow.

On a knoll, he stopped for breath and turned to look. Fire spewed out of both of the barn's loft doors. It had already eaten through the roof. The spreading flames illuminated an area a quarter mile across, including all the ranch buildings. Figures were running in and out of the barn, releasing horses, saving haying machinery and tools. As Holley watched, the floor of the loft collapsed into the barn itself and a shower of sparks erupted from the doors.

Turning, he headed straight across country toward Jed's homestead claim, traveling as swiftly as possible.

A moon was rising when he reached the place. Embers still glowed where the cabin had been. He went to the buggy and unsnapped the weight from the bridle. He climbed to the buggy seat and drove out at a rapid trot toward town.

It was open warfare now. He would be hunted like an animal. The sooner he got his hands on a gun, the better would be his chance of surviving long enough to find out who Jed's killer was.

He reached town shortly before nine o'clock. He drove the buggy into the livery barn and got out of it. The stableman came out of the tackroom, in which a lamp was burning. Holley gave him fifty cents.

He walked uptown toward the sheriff's office. He was ravenous, not having eaten anything all day. But he wanted to see the sheriff first.

Burt Mexico was just locking up. Holley said, "They burned me out."

"Who burned you out?"

"It doesn't matter. You couldn't do anything about it anyway. I haven't any proof."

"Then what do you want from me?"

"A gun. Until the store opens in the morning."

Mexico hesitated. It was too dark for Holley to see his expression but at last the sheriff grunted, "All right. If you'll give me your word you won't go hunting anyone."

Holley said, "You have my word."

"What kind of gun do you want?"

"A double-barreled ten gauge. And some shells with buckshot in them."

"Not taking any chances, are you?"

"I'm not a gunman, Sheriff. If I shoot I want to hit something."

The sheriff went back inside and struck a match. He

lighted the lamp, trimmed the wick, then crossed to the gunrack and took down a gun. He handed it to Holley. From the desk, he took a handful of shells. He handed these to Holley too. "I hope I'm not making a mistake."

Holley didn't answer him. He broke the gun and put two shells into the chambers. He snapped it shut. "Who were the two that had the pitchfork wounds?"

Mexico shook his head. "Forget them. One of them is over at Doc's, in bed. He's in bad shape. The other is back there in a cell."

Holley stared at the sheriff with new respect. "I didn't think you'd do it when the chips were down."

Mexico grinned ruefully. "They wanted me to lock you up instead."

"On what charge?"

"Assault with a deadly weapon. I reminded them that I heard them shooting at you myself."

Holley headed for the door. "I'm going down and get myself something to eat. Want to come along?"

Burt Mexico shook his head. "I don't want to be seen with you. I don't want anyone saying I've taken sides. Besides, I want a drink before I go home."

Holley walked away down the street. The sheriff locked the door of the jail and crossed the street diagonally, heading for the Wild Horse Saloon.

CHAPTER 6

The waitress who had served Holley the night before brought his dinner again tonight. He ate ravenously, paid for the meal, left the restaurant and walked toward the

36

hotel. He couldn't fail to notice the way people he passed in the street avoided his eyes. Nor could he fail to notice the way each of them looked uneasily at the shotgun he was carrying.

The clerk in the hotel acted as if he'd like to refuse Holley a room, but when Holley laid the shotgun on the desk, the man shoved the register at him. Holley signed, picked up the key and went upstairs. He had been assigned the same room he'd had the night before, so he had no trouble finding it.

Inside the room, he locked the door and removed the key. He crossed to the window and stared down into the street. He didn't even know the name of the rancher whose barn he had burned, he thought, and wondered how long it would be before the man came storming into town hunting him.

He took off his boots and stretched out on the bed, reluctant to take off his clothes, reluctant to sleep. He laid the shotgun on the bed beside him, its muzzle pointing toward the door. Inside him the tension was growing steadily. He knew his chances of surviving the next couple of days weren't good. He had deliberately twisted the tiger's tail. Now he must face the tiger's wrath.

He got up nervously and began to pace back and forth. Occasionally he went to the window and stared down into the street. At last his weariness got the best of him and he lay down on the bed. He closed his eyes and was instantly asleep.

It seemed only a minute before he awakened. He lay still, listening, his hand going instinctively to the gun.

Hoofbeats in the street, and shouts, had awakened him. Satisfied that no danger threatened him from inside the hotel, he got up and walked to the window.

Shouting men were clustered in front of the jail. As he watched, a lamp flared inside the place, illuminating those in the street out front.

He recognized Custis, mostly by his size and dress, but he couldn't recognize any of the others. He knew the rancher whose barn he had burned couldn't have trailed him back to Jed's place in the dark. But he also knew the man could have found some of his footprints near the burned-out barn. He could have matched them up with the footprints he'd left at Jed's place earlier. The farmer's shoes were a dead giveaway.

He saw the sheriff come out of the jail and walk toward the hotel. Some of the ranchers started to follow him but he turned and waved them back. He entered the hotel. A few moments later, Holley heard his footsteps in the hall. He crossed to the door and unlocked it. He opened it just as the sheriff knocked.

There was light in the hall, but none in the room. Burt Mexico said reluctantly, "Looks like I've got to arrest you, Holley."

"Why? For burning that rancher's barn? I told you he burned me out first."

Mexico shook his head. "It isn't that. I've got to arrest you for murder."

"Whose murder? What are you talking about?"

"That rancher whose barn you burned. His name was Al Slonicker. He was clubbed to death with a rock not a quarter of a mile from his burning barn. His family and half a dozen others insist that I arrest you and throw you into jail."

Holley said, "I didn't do it, sheriff. I burned the barn, but I didn't kill anybody."

"If you didn't, then you've got nothing to worry about."

Holley stared at him. "You must be out of your mind. A homesteader couldn't get a fair trial here."

"You won't be tried here. I'll take you over to Fairplay. The circuit judge is due there day after tomorrow."

Holley stared at him suspiciously. "And where will you get the jurymen?"

"From the miners over there. These people won't have a thing to do with it."

"Once you arrest me and take this gun, what's to prevent them from breaking into the jail and lynching me?"

Mexico's eyes flared. "I'll prevent them. Now give me the gun."

For an instant, Holley hesitated. Mexico said, "Don't try it. You couldn't get out of this hotel. There are men in

38

front and men in back. If they get you, they'll string you up. Your only chance is to go out of here with me."

Holley stared bleakly at him. He had the sudden feeling that he had lost. He had taken on the whole community and he had lost. He should have known he would.

He handed the shotgun to the sheriff. "Wait until I put on my shoes."

He went back into the room, sat down and put on his shoes. The sheriff waited at the door. Holley said, "You've got no way of knowing that I didn't kill Slonicker, but I know it. So if I didn't kill him, who did? And why? Those people on Shavano Creek wouldn't kill him just so they could accuse me of it. There had to be another reason. Someone had to want him dead. Any ideas who that might be?"

Mexico said, "I'll think on it."

"I sure as hell hope you do. What kind of evidence have they got that it was me?"

"Motive. He burned your shack. Opportunity. They found your tracks near the burned barn. That fight you put up at the stable last night won't help your case. But Judge Myer is fair. He'll listen with an open mind."

Holley shrugged. He got up, walked to the door and out into the hall. The sheriff followed, the shotgun in his hands.

Holley went down the stairs. He started across the lobby but the clerk called out, "What about your room, Mr. Holley? You didn't pay for it."

Holley turned and crossed to the desk. He paid for the room, then went out into the street. The sheriff followed him.

There were now thirty or forty men outside. They began to yell when they saw Holley. "Let's string him up. Let's show these sod-busting sons-of-bitches that they can't come in here and murder the people that live here and get away with it."

Mexico ignored them. He shoved the shotgun muzzle against Holley's back and marched him down the street toward the jail. The mob closed in behind, shouting insults.

Holley turned his head and glared at them but he didn't

say anything. This wasn't exactly the time for threats and defiance. The sheriff was going to have his hands full controlling this mob and there was no use in his making the job more difficult. The sheriff had said he would get a fair trial but somehow or other, Holley was not convinced. Jed hadn't gotten a fair shake here. So far, neither had he. He'd been set upon last night in the livery barn. He'd seen Jed's shack burned. Now he was falsely accused of murder and would be forced to stand trial for it.

The sheriff unlocked the jail door and pushed him inside. He pulled the door shut behind him and shot the bar. He said, "Go on back and pick out a cell."

In one, a man sat on the edge of the cot, his hair mussed, his face haggard and drawn with pain. One leg of his pants had been slit to the thigh and there was a bulky white bandage where the pitchfork tine had entered it. He glared at Holley malevolently.

Holley went into a cell across the corridor. He pulled the door shut. A moment later the sheriff came back and locked it. He pocketed the key.

Holley lay down on the cot. He could still hear the men yelling in the street. He pulled his watch from his pocket and looked at it. It read 2:45.

He closed his eyes. He couldn't sleep but he was determined not to let anyone know how scared he was. The sheriff had said he would be tried by a jury of miners in a town called Fairplay. But even with an impartial jury, he knew how damning the evidence was. He had come here to avenge his brother's death. He had been beaten and his cabin had been burned. His tracks had led to Al Slonicker's place and they'd have no trouble proving not only that he had been there but that he had burned Slonicker's barn. The prosecution would say he had been interrupted by Slonicker in the act and that he had killed Slonicker while making good his escape.

He wasn't stupid and he wasn't gullible. He knew that the jury would probably convict him. The judge would sentence him to hang.

The man across the corridor lay down on his cot with a

groan of pain. The noise in the street in front of the jail slowly diminished.

Slowly the sky outside the jail turned gray. The windows became visible as squares of dingy light. Across the corridor, the wounded man stirred in his sleep, and groaned.

A noise made Holley glance at the window of the cell across the corridor. Briefly he saw a face appear in the rain-spotted window. It disappeared almost as quickly as it had appeared.

Frowning, he waited. The window had been too dirty for him to recognize the man, and he probably wouldn't have recognized him anyway. He had seen a crop of untidy whiskers but that had been about all he'd seen.

Several minutes passed. Suddenly he heard a noise at the window of his own cell. He crossed to it and opened the window. He was aware that the man outside might be planning to kill him in his cell. He was also aware that the safest place would be against the wall immediately beneath the window. The bars would prevent any intruder from getting his head far enough inside to see him crouched down against the wall.

He had never seen the man who stood outside looking in. The man's voice was hoarse and he spoke in a whisper. "I'm Pete Hennies. I knew your brother. I'm pulling out and leaving my homestead, but . . ." He pushed an old, rusty revolver in through the bars. "This ain't much good but it'll shoot. You'd better get out of there because they'll sure string you up if you don't."

Holley took the gun. The man's face disappeared. There was a rustling in the weeds beside the jail and then silence. Holley glanced over his shoulder toward the cell across the corridor as he silently pushed the window closed. The man on the other bunk did not appear to have moved.

Holley looked carefully at the rusty revolver, keeping his body between the man across the corridor and the gun. It was an old percussion piece of uncertain origin. There were caps on the nipples and loads in the cylinder. The walnut grips were gone and the gun squeaked when he pulled the hammer back. He released the hammer carefully and shoved the gun down into his belt. He pulled his coat over it and sat down on his cot. It wasn't much but it was probably enough. He could intimidate the sheriff with it, and he could get a better gun on his way out of the jail.

But he had better act right away. The streets were apparently deserted or Hennies wouldn't have dared bring him the gun.

He yelled, "Sheriff!"

There was only silence. He yelled again. The door leading to the sheriff's office opened and a drowsy Burt Mexico asked, "What do you want?"

"I want some water."

"Can't it wait?"

"Maybe. But you're awake now. How about it?"

"Oh hell, all right. Just a minute." He withdrew into the office, leaving the door ajar. A moment later he reappeared, carrying a bucket and a dipper. He came to Holley's cell door and filled the dipper. Holley hoped the cell key was still in the sheriff's pocket. If it wasn't, he had lost. He reached out for the dipper with one hand. With the other, he drew the gun. The sound of the hammer coming back was a shrill squeak, followed by a click. Holley said, "Don't move, Sheriff. I don't want to shoot you, but I figure I'm going to hang if I don't get out of here."

"You won't get a mile. They'll be after you like a pack of wolves. Can't you see that this is exactly what they want? They can shoot you down and there won't be a damn thing the law can do to them."

"You figure I've got a better chance standing trial?"

The sheriff shrugged. "Any chance is better than none at all."

"Open the cell door, Sheriff." He jabbed with the gun muzzle as he spoke.

Mexico fumbled in his pocket for the key. For an instant it seemed to Holley that he intended to resist. Then, with a little shrug, he withdrew the key from his pocket and inserted it in the lock. "They'll say I let you go."

"No they won't. I'll leave this old gun on your desk."

The door swung open and Holley stepped out into the

42

corridor. The man in the other cell woke up and began to yell. Holley said urgently. "Get in here, Sheriff, and hurry up. I'm about out of time."

Mexico stepped into the cell and Holley drew the door closed. He locked it swiftly and went into the sheriff's office. He threw the rusty revolver on the sheriff's desk. He snatched up a shotgun and got a box of shells from the desk.

He stepped out into the cold gray of early dawn, glanced up and down the street, then headed for the livery stable at a run.

CHAPTER 7

Holley reached the livery stable without seeing anyone. It was still too early, he supposed, for anyone to be on the street. He ducked inside the place and stood there for a moment, breathing hard, feeling unaccustomed tremors in his legs and arms. He was scared. There was no use denying that. He was worse scared than ever before in his life.

So far he had done practically nothing right. He hadn't found out who Jed's killer was. The shack was gone, and with it his carpetbag and all his clothes. He had escaped from jail and made himself a fugitive, whom anyone could shoot on sight with impunity. He had even alienated the sheriff, who previously had been cautiously on his side.

The trouble was, he hadn't been given any choice. The initiative had been taken out of his hands from the moment of his arrival here. Now, he was only doing his best to regain it. If he stayed in jail he was certain to be convicted of killing Slonicker. No jury in its right mind could decide otherwise.

Aware that he had no time to waste, he hurried along the main alleyway of the livery barn until he found a stall with a horse in it. He bridled the animal and led him to the tackroom, where he threw a saddle on. He was thinking that now there would be another charge against him in addition to murder and breaking jail. He was a horse thief too.

He led the horse to the front door of the stable and glanced up and down the street. He saw no one so he mounted and rode out, immediately turning toward the lower end of town. At the first opportunity, he turned west so as to get off the main street and out of sight.

He found the road leading up the valley of Shavano Creek. He hadn't the slightest idea where he was going or what he was going to do.

He thought of Pete Hennies, who had abandoned his homestead and was leaving the valley of Shavano Creek. Hennies hadn't had the courage to stay, but he'd had sufficient courage to slip Holley a gun. Holley was thankful to him for that.

Suddenly he found himself thinking about the Nordlanders. Lars Nordlander had told him to count on them. He had promised help.

If he went there, he could get some food and other supplies. He could get information, vital information that he had to have. Someone had murdered Al Slonicker. Someone had hated him enough to want him dead, enough to batter his head in with a rock. Maybe Lars Nordlander could tell him who hated Slonicker that much.

Clear of the town, he left the road. He climbed his horse through the scrub sagebrush and twisted cedars that covered the hills on both sides of the valley. He knew he couldn't afford to risk traveling on the road.

He wasn't used to riding, but neither was he a complete stranger to it. He kept a wary eye on the valley below, staying out of sight of it as much as possible. He passed the blackened remains of Jed's shack and not long afterwards sighted the Nordlander place.

A draw led down toward it and he put his horse into the concealment of the draw. When he reached the open fields,

44

he kicked the animal's ribs with his heels, forcing him to lope. He pulled up in the brushy creek bottom, dismounted and tied the horse. Afterwards, he approached on foot, after first scanning the yard to be sure there were no saddle horses or strangers visible.

It was still very early, but the sun had poked above the line of mountains east of the Arkansas. It now touched the high peaks and the highest of the hills bordering the valley of Shavano Creek. The door of the Nordlander house opened and Lars Nordlander came out, a bucket in each hand.

Holley stepped into sight. Nordlander glanced at him without apparent surprise. Holley walked toward him and took one of the buckets. He said, "I'll help you milk. I've got to talk to you."

He followed Nordlander into the barn, found a stool and sat down to milk. It was a familiar and pleasant chore, one he suddenly discovered he had missed. He said, "I don't know whether you heard or not, but I was arrested for killing Al Slonicker last night. Pete Hennies slipped me a gun through the cell window and I escaped a while ago."

"You didn't . . . ?"

"Shoot the sheriff? No. He's all right. But I've got to know some things. I've got to know who hated Al Slonicker enough to want him dead. I know I didn't kill him but I'm the only one who does."

"That was Jed's shack burning yesterday, wasn't it? And you burned Slonicker's barn afterward?"

"Uh huh." He finished milking and stood up.

Nordlander said, "What are you going to do?"

Holley followed him out of the barn, the bucket in his hand. "Try to find out who did kill Slonicker, I suppose. I haven't got much choice. If I let them try me for killing him, I'm almost certain to get hanged. I burned his barn and left a lot of tracks. I had a reason and an opportunity."

Nordlander held the door for him and he stepped into the house. Gerda Nordlander glanced around from the stove, her eyes widening with surprise. The children were not present and Holley supposed they were still asleep.

He put the bucket of milk on the table. There was a flush

of pleasure on Gerda's face as she brought a cup of coffee to him. Lars Nordlander said, "Fix Mr. Holley something to eat, Gerda, as quickly as you can."

Gerda asked, "Is someone after him?"

Holley grinned. "Everybody is, I guess. I'm supposed to have killed Al Slonicker when I burned his barn. I've broken out of jail and sooner or later there will be a posse after me."

"What are you going to do?" Her face had turned very pale.

"Stay away from them as long as possible. Try to find out who really killed Slonicker."

She said, "The Custis brothers hated him. They were always fighting over water from the ditch."

Holley glanced at Lars, who nodded agreement. Lars said, "Several months ago, Al Slonicker hit Ben Custis with a shovel and pushed him into the ditch. I think Custis would have drowned if his brother Lance hadn't arrived and pulled him out."

"Then maybe Custis . . ."

Nordlander nodded. "Maybe. But I don't know how you'll find out for sure. They certainly aren't going to admit anything."

"What about tracks?"

"I doubt if you'll find any tracks. The Custis brothers are too smart to leave anything that would lead the sheriff to them."

Gerda had been working swiftly at the stove. Now she brought Holley a plate of food. He sat down and ate hungrily. Nordlander had found a gunny sack and was hastily stuffing things into it.

Holley finished eating and gulped what was left of his coffee. "I don't want to put you in danger. I'll leave right away."

Nordlander said, "Now I am ashamed." He looked straight into Holley's eyes. "I was thinking of Gerda and the children, not of myself."

Holley was embarrassed by Nordlander's embarrassment and didn't know what to say. He said, "Do you have a horse? I stole the one I'm riding but if he was to be turned loose to make his way back to town, at least I wouldn't have that charge hanging over me."

"Of course. I'll go saddle one." Nordlander went outside.

Gerda came to Holley and refilled his cup. He could feel her standing close to him. He could sense that she wanted to say something to him, something she felt was important. But she didn't speak. She returned to the stove and put the coffee pot down again.

He asked, "Did you know Jed well?"

She smiled. "Pretty well, I suppose. We didn't see much of him. He was working hard most of the time, fencing and building that little house."

"Did he have a decent burial?"

"Yes. There was a funeral at the church. It wasn't very well attended, but Lars and I were there. And Pete Hennies and his wife. And the sheriff and Dr. Rounds."

"Who . . . ?"

"Paid for it? The county, I suppose."

There was a long silence. At last Holley said bluntly what was in his mind. "It's unusual to find a woman as young as yourself married to a man Mr. Nordlander's age."

He glanced up at her. Her face was flushed. He asked, "Are the children his?"

"You have no right . . ." She stopped.

He agreed. "No, I guess not. I'm sorry."

With her back to him, she said softly, "The children aren't his. He is a fine man, who married me because I needed someone to take care of me. But we are not . . ." She stopped, turned and looked squarely at him. "We are not really man and wife. He is like a father or a grandfather to me."

Holley turned his head and saw Nordlander approaching, leading a saddled horse. He rose. "I've got to go. I've already been here too long."

She nodded, unspeaking, her glance holding his. He said, "I'm glad you told me."

He stepped out the door and took the reins from Nordlander. He mounted. Nordlander said, "I released your horse and started him down the road toward town."

47

"Won't he be trailed back here?"

Nordlander shook his head. "The road is hard. He will leave no tracks that can be recognized."

Holley nodded. "Thank you. And thank you for the food." He smiled at Gerda, who had come to the door. He rode back toward the creek, the same way he had come earlier.

There was a kind of bleak uncertainty in him. Gerda and Lars Nordlander had offered help but he knew he couldn't bring his trouble to them. Nor could he count on help from Burt Mexico. The sheriff was probably mad enough by now to put him in a cell and throw away the key.

The sun climbed slowly across the sky. Holley headed up through the sagebrush-covered hills, angling toward the upper end of the Slonicker place. What might be accomplished by watching the Custis brothers he had no idea. But it was the only thing left that he could do.

He found himself thinking of Gerda Nordlander. He remembered the way she had looked, standing in the doorway as he rode away, her hand raised to shield her eyes from the sun. He shook his head irritably. He had no right to think of her this way. She was Lars Nordlander's wife, married to him. It was not his business what their relationship was.

But he couldn't stop his thoughts. And he couldn't stop his memories. Her likeness was burned upon his brain. It would come back to haunt him whenever there was a quiet time.

CHAPTER 8

Approaching the Custis place from downcountry, Holley was careful to keep a screen of cedars or brush between him and the ranch buildings most of the time. Whenever this was impossible, he dropped back behind the crest of the nearest ridge, so that he would not be seen.

At last he reached a vantage point that suited him. He led his horse back into some cedars and tied the reins to a branch. Returning, he settled down behind a clump of sagebrush. He stared at the Custis ranch below.

It was considerably bigger than Slonicker's. At least there were more buildings and for the most part they were larger ones. There was a log barn that must have been a hundred and fifty feet long, and there were at least a dozen smaller buildings. The corrals looked as if they'd hold a thousand cattle comfortably.

But there was a run-down look about the place that he hadn't noticed at Slonicker's. A huge pile of discarded tin cans rested not fifty feet from the house. There was a pile of old hides and bones close to the cans. Outside the kitchen door was a spot twenty feet across that was white from a thousand dishpans full of soap suds that had been thrown out the door, and damp from being repeatedly wetted down.

The place said just one thing to Holley. It said "bachelor outfit" as plainly as if there had been a sign. There was either no woman living in the Custis house or else the woman who lived there was as slovenly as the men.

Holley squinted his eyes slightly against the glare of the

49

sun. A couple of pigs prowled the Custis yard, sniffing and rooting where the dishwater had been thrown. Some scraggly-looking white chickens scratched in the two pigs' wake.

The house was a great three-story affair built of logs. They were hand-hewn logs and were chinked with clay. The roof was thatched with hand-split cedar shakes that had obviously been there as long as the house. Whoever built it, thought Holley, had taken a great deal of pains. He had built for the future and what he had built had been intended to stand long after he and his children were dead.

But whoever had inherited the place didn't care the way the original builder had. A window was broken in the house. It had been covered with boards nailed across it on the inside. Chinking had come out from between the logs and no one had bothered to rechink the cracks. The back porch had broken boards in it and broken steps. Trash littered the yard.

A man came out of the house. He was instantly recognizable to Holley as Ben Custis, who had visited him in his hotel room his first night here. Custis walked across the yard to the corral. He entered, took down a rope from the corral fence and caught himself a horse. He threw saddle and blanket onto the horse, also taking these from the corral fence.

Holley could see a ditch bordering the hayfields on this side of the creek. Following the ditch with his gaze, he saw a dam across the creek about a mile and a half upstream from the house. The ditch ran downcountry, where it also bordered Slonicker's place. On the far side of the creek was another ditch which took its water from the same dam but on the other side.

Those must be the ditches the Custis family and the Slonickers had fought about, he thought.

Two more men came from the house. One of them went to the corral and caught two horses. They were bigger horses than Ben Custis had caught, either work or wagon horses. He led them into the barn. He was gone ten or fifteen minutes. When he emerged, he was driving them, harnessed now. He drove them to a wagon and backed

50

them into position, one on each side of the wagon tongue. He hitched them up, then drove the wagon to the house. He and the other man began to carry out blocks of salt and to load the wagon with them.

Holley supposed the house was chiefly used for storage now. He could imagine the dining room and living room, bare of furniture, piled high with great quantities of supplies, of salt, of barbed wire. The brothers probably had bedrooms upstairs. Their leisure time, what there was of it, was most likely spent in the kitchen beside the stove.

How in the hell, wondered Holley, was he going to prove from here that one of the Custis brothers had killed Al Slonicker? He couldn't hear what they were saying. He couldn't see the expressions their faces wore. All he could see was what they were doing and that wasn't going to tell him anything.

He fished a cigar from his pocket and stuck it into his mouth without lighting it. He chewed the end of it thoughtfully. How long could he avoid the posse that was sure to be chasing him? How long could he outguess men who had been raised in this country and knew it like they knew the backs of their hands?

A movement in the direction of Slonicker's place caught his wary eye and he glanced that way. He saw nothing, but he nevertheless continued to watch. After a long time he caught the flash of movement again. This time he saw what it was: the brown rump of a horse, briefly visible where there was a break in the screen of brush.

A frown touched his forehead. It wasn't natural for a loose horse to move as fast as this one was moving. Holley guessed that someone had to be leading the animal.

His eyes calm but somewhat worried, he shifted the shotgun into a better position across his knees. Several moments later he caught a glimpse of a man. The man disappeared and a moment later Holley saw the brown horse again. Man and horse were now no more than a quarter mile away.

The man couldn't be tracking him, Holley thought. He hadn't even come that way. And since the man was downhill from him and not headed toward him, it followed

51

that the man didn't realize he was here.

Then what *was* the man following? His heart began to thump harder in his chest. Tracks? Tracks leading from Slonicker's barn toward the Custis place?

Suddenly the man stepped into the open. He was only visible to Holley an instant, but it was enough. The man was Burt Mexico. And he was following a trail. He seemed oblivious of everything else and he did not glance up.

Holley hesitated for several moments. He was intensely curious about the trail the sheriff was following. He also realized that if this first guess had been correct, then he had better go down and give the sheriff a hand.

He got up carefully and eased back through the brush to where he had left his horse. He untied him and, picking a way through the heaviest brush he could find, headed downhill toward Burt Mexico.

It was impossible to travel without making a great deal of noise. Grinning ruefully, Holley followed a course that he had calculated would intersect the sheriff's course. As long as he was making all this noise at least he wasn't going to startle Mexico and get shot by mistake.

But he wondered how Burt Mexico would react to him. He had stuck a gun into the sheriff's ribs and had forced him to unlock the cell. He had locked Mexico in and it must have been very embarrassing for the sheriff to have people find him locked up in one of his own jail cells.

He came face to face with the sheriff suddenly. Mexico stood with his horse in a small clearing. There was a rifle in his hands and it was pointed straight at Holley's chest. Holley said, "No use being soreheaded, Sheriff. You'd have done the same thing if you'd been in my shoes."

Mexico scowled at him. He said, "Drop the shotgun. Now."

Holley shook his head. "Huh uh. I didn't walk all the way down this hill just to give myself up to you. I could have stayed up there out of sight."

The two stared warily at each other. Holley asked, "What are you doing, anyway? Following a trail?"

The sheriff nodded. "I figured whoever killed Slonicker

might have been so damned sure you'd be blamed that he might have gotten careless about his tracks. So I made a circle around the place and sure enough, I picked them up. That's what I'm following and it looks like the trail's heading straight toward the Custis place."

"Will that prove anything?"

"Not unless we find the horse in Custis's corral. But the horse can be identified. He ain't shod and there's a big crack in the hoof of his right forefoot."

"Were you able to tell how old the tracks were?"

"Near enough. It rained the night before you came. At least it'll throw doubt on the idea that you killed Slonicker. Everybody knows about the trouble between Slonicker and the Custis family."

"You're not going down there alone?"

"That's what the county pays me for."

"What's to keep them from killing you?"

Mexico shrugged. "Let me worry about that. You wait here. I'll want you to come back to town with me."

"What's the matter with me helping you? There are four of them down there. If they're guilty of killing Slonicker, you don't think they're going to let you examine the hoofs of every horse they've got, do you?"

For the first time, a shadow of doubt touched the sheriff's face. At last he nodded reluctantly. He said, "All right. You work your way into the creek bottom and approach from that direction so you won't be seen. Go into the barn first and look at the right front hoofs of any horses that are there. I'll follow this trail as far as I can, right into the yard if that's where it goes."

"What if the horse isn't in the barn?"

"Then maybe he'll be in the corral. But if you don't find him, leave the same way you came, without being seen. Will you agree to that?"

Holley nodded.

"All right then, get going. I'll give you a start of about ten minutes. Watch for me and don't go into the barn until you see me ride into the yard. I can distract them long enough to give you a chance to look for the horse."

53

Holley started away, leading his horse. The sheriff said, "Don't take your horse. Tie him here and come back for him."

Holley nodded and tied the horse. He started away but the sheriff asked, "What did you do with the horse you stole?"

Holley swung his head and grinned. "Me steal a horse?"

"Where'd you get that one?"

"Lars Nordlander loaned him to me."

"And I suppose you walked all the way to Nordlander's from town?"

Holley didn't answer him and it was apparent the sheriff didn't care. He headed away downhill through the brush, careful to keep his body screened from the Custis place whenever possible.

He reached the ditch at the edge of the wide hayfield. Fortunately, the barn was now between him and the big log house. He ran across the field, his head turned toward the house, ready to drop should any of the four Custis brothers appear.

He reached the creek, sweating and out of breath. He took a moment to catch his breath before going on.

Here the creek made a roar that drowned out all other sounds. Not bothering to be quiet any longer, he hurried toward the towering barn, the top of which was visible above the brush and trees.

A part of the creek was fenced into the corral so that cattle and horses held in the corral could drink at will. Holley climbed through the fence and ran swiftly to the barn.

He eased open the door but it creaked thunderously anyway. Once inside, he froze for a moment, listening.

He was under no illusions as to what would happen to him if he was found in here. He would be shot on sight. Not only could the Custis brothers say they had thought he meant to burn their barn too. They could also say they were only shooting down a murderer.

He heard no sounds not made by the horses in their stalls so he crossed the barn swiftly and peered out a window on the other side.

54

The sheriff was just now riding into the yard, still following the trail. Apparently it was lost in other tracks immediately, because Mexico glanced up.

The Custis brothers, all four of them, stood before the back door of the house. Mexico rode across the yard toward them. Without waiting to see what would happen, Holley turned and headed for the nearest stall.

CHAPTER 9

He was very conscious of the need for haste. He didn't know how long the sheriff would be able to stall the Custis brothers out there in the yard. Their attitude had been visibly hostile as Mexico approached.

He slid into the stall with the first horse he reached, a bay gelding, and lifted the animal's forefoot to look at it. The light inside the barn was poor, but even in poor light he could tell the hoof had no crack in it.

Swiftly he moved on to the next horse, a dappled gray. Again the hoof was unblemished. The third horse was shod. The fourth, a sorrel, had the split hoof he was looking for.

He untied the horse's halter rope and backed him out of the stall. Leading the horse, he headed for the door.

The Custis brothers did not immediately see him as he came out of the barn but the sheriff did. He looked at Holley questioningly and Holley nodded. Ben Custis caught the direction of the sheriff's glance and turned. He started visibly when he saw Holley with the horse. His hand moved toward his gun.

Mexico's voice was like a whip. "Ben! Don't!"

Holley's shotgun was negligently held, its barrel resting on his left forearm. His right hand was on the receiver, the forefinger on the trigger. He had dropped the horse's halter rope, and the animal stood motionless behind him in the doorway of the barn. He said, "This thing will spray considerably at this range. It would probably get all four of you."

Ben Custis's hand rested a moment on the grips of his gun. Then he lifted it carefully away. He looked at the sheriff and growled, "What the hell is *he* doing here?"

"He's helping me. And it looks like he found what he was looking for."

"And that was?"

"A horse with a split hoof." Mexico looked at Holley. "Bring him over here. I want to see what his hoof print looks like."

Without taking his eyes off the Custis brothers and without changing the direction in which the shotgun pointed, Holley picked up the horse's reins and led him across the yard. He led him past, close to the sheriff, and Mexico looked down at the prints he had left in the deep, dry dust. He nodded. "That's him."

"What the hell do you mean, that's him?" Ben Custis's voice was both angry and arrogant, but Holley thought he detected a false note in it.

"That's the horse I trailed from Al Slonicker's place. What I want to know now is which one of you was riding him."

"How the hell do I know who was riding him? We ride whichever horse is handy at the time. And besides, what difference does it make? We ride down to Slonicker's a couple of times a week. The son-of-a-bitch keeps stealing water out of our ditch."

"Is that why he was killed?"

"You know why he was killed. This nester killed him for burning that slab shack down there on his brother's homestead claim."

"That isn't what the tracks say, Ben. I trailed your horse from the spot Al Slonicker was found."

"You found his tracks too, didn't you?"

56

"Not near the body, Ben. The only tracks I found there were boot tracks. The kind of boots you and your brothers wear."

Ben Custis snorted angrily.

Mexico said, "Which one of you was it, Ben? Which one of you rode this sorrel the day Slonicker was killed?"

Holley was staring toward the four, glancing from one face to another. The sheriff was also staring steadily at them. The silence dragged. Ben Custis glared back defiantly. The sheriff asked deliberately, "What about it, Ralph? Were you riding the sorrel last?"

The man standing next to Ben, apparently only a year or so younger than he, shook his head. Mexico glanced at the next one in line. "Mark?"

"Not me." Mark turned his head and looked at Ben. "What the hell are we standing here letting that bastard question us for anyway? He ain't got no right to come barging in here accusing us of things like that."

Mexico ignored the outburst. He looked at the last of the Custis brothers, apparently the youngest of the four. "Lance? Were you riding the sorrel? Did you kill Al Slonicker?"

Lance glared at the sheriff defiantly. Again the silence dragged for what seemed an interminable interval. Then Lance Custis's glance fell away from the sheriff's and he began to sweat. Mexico said, "That's what I want to know. I'm taking you in for murder, Lance."

Ben's voice was an angry roar. "The hell you are! I'll kill you before I'll let you take Lance away!"

Holley's finger tightened on the trigger of the shotgun. He wondered if he could really fire it, at this close range, knowing it would kill all four of the men facing him. He tried not to let any doubt show in his face. The sheriff said, "Holley, if any one of them grabs for his gun, shoot. You understand?"

Holley nodded. He and the sheriff remained silent and motionless for a moment, then the sheriff said, "Lance, lead that horse back into the barn and throw a saddle on. You're going to Wild Horse to jail."

Lance turned his head and glanced beseechingly at Ben.

Ben was scowling but he nodded his head at Lance. "Do it for now. They've got us cold. But it ain't always going to be this way."

Lance left his brothers and approached Holley reluctantly. Holley released the reins and stepped back away from him, keeping the shotgun trained on the remaining three. Lance reached the horse and picked up the reins.

Both Holley and the sheriff continued to watch the remaining brothers, alert for that slight expression change that would signal their intention to resist. Burt Mexico said softly, "Keep that shotgun on them. I'll go into the barn with Lance."

"All right."

"If they try anything, you shoot. If you don't, you'll sure be dead. Ben gets his gun out fast and he hits whatever he shoots it at."

Holley nodded. He realized that his knees were trembling and he hoped the Custis brothers couldn't see. He'd been in the army during the war but he'd never been closer to the fighting than a mile or two. He'd certainly never faced armed men with a gun in his hands.

The sheriff and Lance were gone for what seemed like a long, long time. Actually, Holley supposed it couldn't have been more than a minute or two. At last Lance came out leading the sorrel, saddled now. The sheriff followed half a dozen steps behind.

Mexico walked to his horse, picked up the reins and swung astride. He rode to Holley and reached down for the gun. Holley handed it to him. Mexico covered the Custis brothers with it. He said, "Get up behind me. We'll ride double to where we left your horse."

Holley put a foot into the stirrup and swung up awkwardly. The sheriff said, "Get my revolver out of the holster and hold it on Lance."

Holley obeyed. The sheriff kicked the horse into motion, turning his body as the horse moved away. As they neared the limit of the shotgun's range, he called back, "Ben, if you start shooting at us, I start shooting at Lance."

The Custis brothers remained in the yard looking

58

sullenly after them. Only when they were safely out of a rifle's range did the sheriff let himself relax. He called directions to Lance, ahead, and Lance followed them. A few minutes later they reached the place where Holley had left his horse.

He slid off, untied the horse and mounted him. He exchanged guns with the sheriff. Mexico said, "Head for town, Lance. Stay ahead of us and don't try to run."

Lance didn't reply, but his horse moved out, heading down through the sagebrush toward the road. Mexico let him get twenty or thirty feet ahead.

Holley said softly, "They'll come after him, won't they?"

Burt Mexico nodded.

"And what will you do then?"

The sheriff turned his head. "What I'm paid to do, I guess."

"What about the rest of the cowmen on Shavano Creek?"

"They'll most likely take sides with the Custis brothers."

"Why? Didn't they like Slonicker?"

"No, but it isn't entirely that. They'll figure I'm taking sides with the homesteaders by letting you off the hook and jailing Lance."

"Can Lance be convicted?"

"I doubt it. I doubt if we can get a jury from people in this county that will convict him."

"Then why bring him to trial?"

"That's a funny question for you to ask. Last night you were in jail on the same murder charge. Trying Lance will get you off the hook. But that ain't really why I'm doing it." Mexico glanced at Holley stubbornly. "I'm doing it because it's right. Lance killed Slonicker. I know it, even if the charge won't stand up in court."

Holley felt a stir of admiration for the sheriff's stubbornness. Mexico knew how dangerous it was to buck the Custis family. He knew he would probably fail in his attempt to make Lance pay for killing Slonicker. But he was trying anyway.

The miles passed slowly beneath their horses' hoofs. Lance Custis rode with his head down on his chest,

59

obviously depressed and deep in thought. He made no attempt to escape, probably counting on his brothers to get him safely out of his predicament.

Holley had the disquieting feeling that he was sinking ever more deeply into the trouble that stalked this country the way a hunter stalks his kill. He had the feeling that he had become the catalyst, the ingredient necessary to make the smoldering hatreds here explode into open violence.

He also knew that when the explosion came, he might be the first to die in it. He might never know who had killed Jed.

But he also realized something else, realized it suddenly and with a touch of surprise. He had come to find out who killed Jed, but that was no longer his only reason for staying on. With each day, with each hour that passed, he became more deeply involved personally with the people here. He incurred debts and loyalties. He owed the sheriff something for his undeviating honesty, which had cleared him at least temporarily of the murder charge. He owed Lars Nordlander, and Gerder, and he experienced a guilty excitement just thinking about her.

He was a fool and he ought to leave at once. There was nothing here in the valley of Shavano Creek for him. Nothing but dishonor and maybe death. Gerda was married to Lars Nordlander. Nothing was going to change that fact.

He saw the town of Wild Horse ahead. At the edge of it, the sheriff closed the interval between the two of them and Lance.

When they reached the jail, Lance swung off his horse. Mexico took him inside, turning his head in the doorway to say, "Take the horse to the stable, will you Mr. Holley?"

Holley nodded. Leading the sheriff's horse and Lance's, he headed for the livery barn. He wondered what was going to happen next.

CHAPTER 10

The stableman glared angrily at Holley when he walked into the livery barn. "You sure as hell have got a nerve! You steal a horse from me and then you come walkin' in here as bold as brass like you hadn't done anything!"

Holley glanced along the line of stalls. He saw the horse he had ridden out of town this morning standing in one of them. "He came home, didn't he? Besides, I didn't steal him. I rented him. You just didn't happen to be here and I couldn't wait."

The man took the reins of the three horses from him sullenly. Holley said, "The Nordlander horse is mine. The sorrel belongs to Lance Custis and the other one is the sheriff's horse."

"I know Burt's horse without you tellin' me."

Holley gave him a half dollar and left, heading along the street toward the jail. Mexico obviously expected trouble from the Custis brothers. Holley wondered how long it would be before they arrived in town.

It was mid-afternoon. He passed several people in the street. They all seemed to know who he was. None spoke, but they watched him suspiciously. Probably surprised, he thought, to see him free after breaking out of jail early this morning and locking the sheriff up in one of his own jail cells.

He went into the jail. The man he had stabbed in the thigh with the pitchfork the night of his arrival was yelling that he wanted the doctor right away. He claimed that he had blood poisoning. His leg was swelling up.

61

Mexico went to the door leading to the cells and opened it. "Shut up, Trimmer. I sent someone after Doc. He'll be here as soon as he can."

Lance Custis said, "You'd better let me go, Burt. Before Ben and the boys get here."

"You shut up too."

"You're really talkin' big, ain't you? Well, go right ahead. Enjoy yourself while you can. You may be dead come night."

"Your brothers aren't coming, Lance. You're going to be tried and you're going to hang."

Custis laughed. It was a nasty laugh that betrayed no fear. He said, "Don't bet your life on it."

Burt Mexico slammed the door. He walked to the window and stared moodily into the street. Without turning he said, "I guess I'm just a plain damn fool. I know I can't keep Lance in jail. If they don't kill me and break him out, he'll be acquitted when he comes to trial. I guess maybe I'm just sick of having the whole county run by the Custis brothers and a few of their friends."

"Do you really think they'll try and break Lance out?"

"Think? Hell, I know they will. And they won't mind killing me to do it, either. Once I'm out of the way, they can put somebody in this job that will do what they tell him to."

"Did one of them kill Jed?"

The sheriff turned his head. "I don't know, Holley. But I'd say they were likely suspects, along with Al Slonicker. Both Al and the Custis brothers wanted the land your brother had. Now that Al is dead I expect Ben Custis will get Slonicker's place from his widow and if he can get rid of you, he'll get your brother's place too."

Holley said suddenly, "How'd you like a deputy?"

"I'd like nothing better." The sheriff turned his head and peered at Holley surprisedly. "You aren't volunteering for the job, are you?"

Holley nodded.

Mexico said, "You're crazy. Why would you want that job?"

"I want to find the man that killed Jed and I want to see him go to trial. It's open season on me anyway as far as the Custis brothers are concerned. Maybe between the two of us, we can give them a fight."

The sheriff did not immediately reply. The door opened and Doc came in. He looked at the sheriff, then at Holley, then back to the sheriff again. "Did you send word that Bus Trimmer wanted me?"

"Uh huh. He claims his leg is swelling up. He thinks he's got blood poisoning."

"Well I can't treat him here in jail. I'll probably have to lance the wound."

"All right, Doc. Take him out. I guess he isn't going anyplace with that leg of his."

"Will you help me get him to the office?"

"Sure." Mexico went back and unlocked Trimmer's cell. He returned with Trimmer, who was leaning heavily on him. Holley held the door. The sheriff, Doc and Trimmer disappeared from his view.

He closed the door. Mexico hadn't said whether he would accept him as a deputy or not, but apparently he trusted him enough to leave him in charge of the jail. He grinned humorlessly to himself. This morning he had been in jail. Then he'd put a gun on the sheriff and broken out. Now he was in charge of the place. Quite a change in a single day.

The sheriff wasn't gone more than five minutes at the most. When he returned, he rummaged in his desk, finally withdrawing a tarnished deputy's badge. He said, "Raise your right hand."

Holley did. Mexico administered the oath and Holley pinned on the badge. Mexico said, "Pay's forty a month. Is that all right?"

Holley nodded. Mexico said, "The first thing we ought to do is eat. Go over to the restaurant and tell 'em we want three meals. You come right back. They'll deliver the food."

Holley nodded. He went out and hurried along the street to the restaurant. The restaurant was serving chicken and

63

dumplings today so he ordered three plates sent down to the jail. He hurried back.

He had his hand on the doorknob when he saw Ben Custis turn the corner onto Shavano Street a block away. He hesitated a moment, waiting to see how many men Ben had with him.

Mark and Ralph rounded the corner behind Ben. Two other men followed.

Holley went into the jail. "The Custis brothers are here. They've got two other men with them. Five in all."

Mexico crossed to the window and glanced out. "The other two are Jess Kellison and Elias Seroco. They're Ben's neighbors on the west." He crossed to the gunrack and took down a double-barreled shotgun. He gestured with his head at Holley's gun leaning against the wall. "Load up. They're coming here."

He stuffed a couple of shells into the gun. Holley picked up his own shotgun, the one Mexico had given him yesterday, and loaded it. Mexico sat down at his desk, the shotgun resting on his knees, pointing at the door. Holley moved to the other side of the room. He sat down in a straight-backed chair, also facing toward the door.

The Custis brothers and their two friends came to a halt in the street before the jail, but only Ben Custis dismounted and came inside. He scowled when he saw Holley. He turned his head and glared at Mexico. "We've come for Lance."

"Then you've wasted a trip. He's staying here until he goes to trial."

"And when will that be?"

"When the judge gets here, probably day after tomorrow."

Ben looked at Holley. "What about him?"

"I've made him my deputy."

For a moment Ben was silent. His face got red and his eyes narrowed. When he spoke, his voice was cold with anger. "God damn you Mexico, this time you've gone too far. This stinkin' nester burned Slonicker's barn. You've got proof of that even if you haven't got proof that he killed

64

Al. Either you put him in jail or I warn you, I'm breaking Lance out of it."

Mexico got up. He walked to Ben Custis and stood facing him. "There's been a showdown building up around here for a long, long time. You and that bunch on Shavano Creek think you're above the law. You think you can do anything, assault, arson, murder, and get away with it. Well maybe you can, but you're going to have to get rid of me first. And if you get rid of me, then Judge Myer is going to be coming in here asking questions. Maybe he'll bring a federal marshal along with him and maybe he won't. But sooner or later you're going to have to face the facts. You're not living on a wild frontier anymore. This is a territory of the United States and you're subject to its laws."

Custis uttered a single, contemptuous obscenity. He glared at the sheriff a moment more, then turned and stalked out of the jail. Those he had left in the street spoke to him. He turned his head and cursed them furiously.

Holley said, "Heated up, isn't he?"

"Uh huh. The hell of it is, with Ben it's not just blow. He's dangerous. He's used to handling things himself."

"What do you think he'll do?"

"Break Lance out of jail." Mexico studied Holley. "I shouldn't have sworn you in as deputy. I knew what Ben would do." He held out a hand. "Give me back the badge. This is my job, not yours."

Holley said, "Maybe with two of us, he'll back off."

"Huh uh. Not Ben."

Holley said, "I think I'll keep the badge."

Mexico shrugged. "Don't say I didn't warn you."

"What's next?"

"Ben probably won't do anything tonight. He'll spend the night in the saloon. By tomorrow, he'll feel mean enough and reckless enough to take on both of us. If one of us was to ride over to Fairplay tonight, we could probably get Judge Myer to come over early tomorrow and start the trial. With the judge in town, maybe Ben would have sense enough to behave himself."

65

Holley grinned slightly. "You're as stubborn as Ben. You know Lance will be acquitted but you've got to try him anyway."

"I want Ben to know that things are going to be done by law. That's all."

Holley said, "You'd better be the one to go over and get the judge. You know the way and you know the judge. I'll stay here and watch the jail."

Mexico said, "All right, if you'll promise me one thing. If Ben and the rest of them come after Lance, you give him up. We can get him back any time we want."

"Would you give him up if you were staying here?"

"That's different. I'm the sheriff and you're not."

Holley hesitated. Mexico said, "I won't go unless you agree."

Holley nodded. "All right. You're the boss."

"Good." Mexico crossed the room and got his hat. He put on a coat, checked the loads in his revolver absentmindedly, then got a Spencer repeating rifle from the rack. He stuffed a box of cartridges for it into the pocket of his coat.

Holley had been watching Ben Custis and those with him as the sheriff talked, but now they had disappeared into the Wild Horse Saloon. Mexico went out and headed down the street toward the livery stable just as the waitress from the restaurant approached the jail, carrying three stacked-up trays.

Seeing her, Mexico came back. He held the door for her and Holley took her trays. Mexico said, "Thanks, Madge."

She nodded and smiled at him. Holley had never seen her smile and was surprised at how much younger it made her look. Mexico closed the door. "I might as well eat before I leave. It'll be a damn long night."

He sat down at his desk and quickly ate the meal. When he had finished, he went again to the door. "Eat that other dinner if you want it, Holley. Trimmer likely won't get back at all tonight."

Holley nodded. The sheriff went out and headed for the livery barn. He disappeared inside and a few moments later emerged. He turned his horse north along Shavano Street and nodded at Holley as he passed the jail.

Holley began to eat his dinner, occasionally glancing out at the saloon. The sheriff had been gone less than five minutes when Ben Custis and his two brothers emerged. They talked together a moment before mounting their horses.

Holley continued to watch them curiously. They rode up the street past the jail, but oddly enough none of the three glanced at it. Holley frowned slightly at their failure to do so because it wasn't natural. They continued on up Shavano Street toward the north, the same direction the sheriff had taken earlier.

Holley crossed to the door and stepped outside. He saw them leave town and take the stage road that followed the valley of the Arkansas.

There could be no doubt where they were going. They must have seen Burt Mexico leave town and they were following. Nor could there be any doubt about what their intentions were. They were going to kill him, ambush him on the trail.

Holley hesitated only a moment. With the Custis brothers out of town, Lance would be safe enough. Besides, Lance wasn't important anymore. Not with the sheriff's life at stake.

He snatched up a rifle and left the jail hurriedly, not even bothering to lock the door. He ran down the street to the livery barn. He told the stableman he wanted the fastest horse he had.

The stableman stared suspiciously at the deputy badge. Holley said impatiently, "Hurry it up, damn it. And if you don't give me a good horse I'm coming back and kick the hell out of you."

The stableman hurried away. When he came back, he was leading a big, leggy roan. Holley swung to the saddle and kicked the horse's sides. The startled horse thundered out of the livery barn and up the street in the same direction the Custis brothers had gone a few minutes earlier.

CHAPTER 11

The sun was now almost directly overhead. Shavano Creek made a steady roar tumbling through town on its way to the Arkansas.

The stable horse slowed almost immediately to a dragging walk and Holley kicked his sides until the animal broke into a reluctant lope. He cursed the stableman sourly. The man's petty vindictiveness in giving him a lazy horse might cost Burt Mexico his life. For several moments he debated turning around and going back for a better horse. He discarded the idea. Going back would consume too much time. He would have to do the best he could with the horse he had.

The road followed the Arkansas for about a dozen miles. Occasionally, in the distance, Holley would see the lift of a cloud of dust. Or from some high point he would see three specks on the road ahead. Occasionally he could also see the tracks of the Custis brothers' horses where the dust in the road was deep enough.

His heels drummed against the roan's sides continuously and angrily. At last, in desperation, he stopped and cut a willow whip. A few sharp blows with the whip convinced the roan that he had better move on out, and he broke into a steady, mile-eating lope. Holley grinned ruefully. The roan was good enough. He was just used to his rider wearing spurs.

The miles began to fall rapidly behind. The road crossed the river on a log bridge and began its winding ascent to the top of Trout Creek Pass. By now, Holley had gained nearly half a mile on the three Custis brothers. Even so, he lost them in the pines immediately after they crossed the bridge.

He wondered if they had seen him following. He also wondered if they would stop and ambush him. He decided that they probably would not. They didn't consider him dangerous enough to worry about and they wouldn't risk losing the sheriff by stopping to ambush him.

The climb was steep and he was forced to halt the horse several times to rest. Even so, sweat soon soaked the horse's neck and shoulders.

A strong smell of pine filled the air up here, combining with the familiar and pungent smell of sage. A bunch of deer stared at him curiously from a clump of aspen trees, then bounded away across the mountain slope.

Climbing steadily, the road went on and on. Since Holley could no longer follow the three ahead of him by sight, he was forced to keep a close eye on the road. In most places it was rocky, but here and there was a damp spot soft enough to retain a horse's tracks, and at each of these places he checked to make sure the Custis brothers were still ahead of him.

Half a dozen miles from the river, their trail unexpectedly left the road. Holley stopped, hesitating, frowning with uncertainty. Here near the top of the pass the land had leveled out somewhat. There were open, grassy meadows beside the road, fringed with aspens and darker spruce.

Of one thing he was sure. The three brothers had not given up their pursuit of Mexico. If they had left the road it could only mean that they meant to get ahead of the sheriff so that they could ambush him.

Having decided he would make better time if he stayed on the road, Holley whipped the roan into a steady run. He had to catch Mexico before he rode into the ambush the brothers were setting up for him.

Excitement now seemed to possess the roan in spite of his weariness. He ran eagerly while Holley leaned low over his neck, reins in one hand, rifle and willow whip in the other. A mile passed, and a second mile.

Suddenly Holley hauled in on the reins. His ears had caught sounds, sounds almost drowned out by the thunder of the horse's hoofs against the rocky road.

The horse came to a plunging halt. The sounds were clearer now—shots from straight ahead, in distance sounding like the popping of firecrackers on Independence Day.

Holley's first inclination was to spur the horse, to try to reach the sheriff as soon as possible, but he realized almost immediately that it would be the most foolish thing he could do. The sheriff was obviously still alive or the shooting would have stopped. He had survived the ambush and had probably taken cover in some rocks or trees. He was fighting back. He might be wounded but he wasn't dead.

Holley let his horse move out at a trot. The shots had been at least a quarter mile away. He could still go quite a way on the road and by doing so make better time.

Gauging his progress by the continuing reports, he finally left the road and entered a thick grove of pines. He tied his horse and went on afoot, climbing but also angling toward the direction from which the shots had come.

He reached a promontory of rock about a hundred and fifty yards above the road. Poking his head up cautiously, he saw puffs of powdersmoke coming from the lower side of the road immediately below his vantage point. He saw the sheriff's horse lying on the road, kicking helplessly, unable to get up. He saw puffs of smoke coming from the guns of two of the Custis brothers, crouched in some more rocks below him on the slope. He caught a glimpse of the third brother circling, trying to reach a vantage point below the road from which he could get a shot at Mexico.

The backs of the two Custis brothers were toward him and less than a hundred yards away. Resting his rifle on a rock, he took a bead on Ben Custis's back.

He squeezed the trigger gently, but at the last minute he moved his point of aim. The gun roared and he saw rock dust spurt less than six inches from Ben Custis's head.

Ben recoiled from the bullet's impact violently, stung by flying rock particles. He whirled and searched the slope

70

behind him. The other brother, Mark, followed suit.

Holley ducked his head and kept it down for what seemed like an eternity. Let them worry about where he was. Let them wonder how many men were here behind them on the slope.

From the side of the road, Burt Mexico's firing had increased its tempo. Holley risked a quick glance over the top of the rock behind which he was concealed.

The two Custis brothers, Ben and Mark, were still in the same place below him in the rocks. The third was moving through the brush behind the sheriff and below the road.

Holley rested his rifle on the rock again. This time he held his point of aim and squeezed his shot off carefully. He was rewarded by a violent flurry of movement in the brush below the road and by a high yell of pain that was a couple of seconds reaching him because of the distance involved. He grinned with satisfaction.

Mexico, suddenly made aware of the man below and behind him in the brush, turned and began firing. Holley caught a glimpse of the wounded brother withdrawing hastily.

What existed now was a stalemate, he thought. There wasn't much chance that the sheriff could get away and go on to Fairplay as long as Ben and Mark were above him in the rocks. He'd have to wait for dark.

But neither was there much chance that the sheriff would be killed. Not as long as Holley stayed up here on the slope. Mark and Ben didn't dare leave the shelter of their rocks. The third brother, Ralph, was wounded and had probably lost all his enthusiasm for the fight.

Holley reached into his pocket for a cigar. Ben and Mark undoubtedly knew where he was by now so the smoke wasn't going to give anything away. He lighted it, leaned back against a rock and puffed nervously.

A sudden flurry of firing made him raise his head. He saw the sheriff just disappearing into the brush a dozen yards below the road. Mexico was bent low and running hard. Bullets kicked up rock dust from the ground in back of him.

Holley opened fire instantly. His bullets ricocheted from

71

the rocks where Ben and Mark were concealed. Their firing stopped as they ducked their heads.

Holley examined the brush below the road carefully. Once he thought he saw movement, but it was soon gone, and he realized that he might have imagined it. Mexico's horse was down and useless in the road. If the sheriff intended to go on to Fairplay, he would have to have another horse.

He was probably trying to reach the horses of the three Custis brothers. Or he might be backtracking, looking for his unexpected ally's horse.

Holley hoped Mexico wouldn't feel reluctant about leaving, and he doubted if the sheriff would. Mexico was a tough and competent man. He might not know who had intervened and made it possible for him to escape, but he wasn't likely to spoil what they had done indulging in heroics. No, he'd go on to Fairplay for the judge. And when darkness came, Holley could escape himself.

Below him, Ben Custis began to bellow. "Ralph! Goddam it, Ralph, where the hell are you? Mexico got away! He's headin' for our horses! We're pinned down but you can stop him! Ralph!"

There was no answer from Ralph. Holley wondered uneasily if Ralph had been more seriously wounded than it had appeared. It was possible, he had to admit. Ralph might be lying down there in the brush someplace, unconscious from loss of blood. Or he might just be too sick to care whether Mexico escaped or not.

On the far side of the valley, Holley suddenly caught a glimpse of a horseman picking his way through the trees. He followed the horseman's progress intently, and when the man emerged briefly into a small clearing, he was able to recognize Burt Mexico. The sheriff disappeared again. Ten minutes later, Holley saw him climb his horse out into the road half a mile above. He was not riding Holley's roan. He must, then, have found the horses of the Custis brothers and taken one of them. He had probably released the others and started them toward home.

Holley couldn't help but grin. Ben Custis was going to be

furious when he found all three of their horses gone. By the time he got back to town . . .

His grin disappeared. There was nothing funny about Ben Custis being furious. Custis was as dangerous a man as Holley had ever seen. There was no telling what he might do.

He settled himself as comfortably as he could so that he could keep an eye on Ben and Mark. A couplt of times they showed signs of trying to leave their cluster of rocks. Both times he laid several shots close enough to change their minds.

The sun slid down the western sky with a slowness that was maddening. Holley kept watching for Ralph, but the man did not appear. He would have a slight edge on the Custis brothers when dark finally came, he thought, because they'd have to locate Ralph before they could leave. That would give him time to find his horse.

Slowly, slowly, the sun sank to the western horizon and dipped its rim. The light scattering of clouds flamed orange, then red. The sun disappeared, throwing shadow over all the land. And with its going, the air chilled immediately.

The Custis brothers had stood up, and now stared toward the place where Holley was concealed. They showed no fear of him, apparently sure he would not fire unless they tried to escape.

Burt Mexico ought to be in Fairplay by now, he thought. He ought to be back in Wild Horse tomorrow with the circuit judge. Lance Custis could go to trial.

Yet somehow he could not make himself believe that Lance Custis would ever go to trial. There was something down there in the valley of Shavano Creek he had encountered nowhere else, ever before. It was a kind of arrogant lawlessness that only time and violence could tame. Ben Custis and a lot of others would have to be He would have been more surprised to find Lance still in the valley of Shavano Creek.

Dusk crept slowly across the land. When he could no longer see the outlines of the two Custis brothers in the rocks, Holley got stiffly to his feet and crept away silently toward his horse. He had gone no more than a couple of hundred yards before he heard Ben Custis bellowing for Ralph.

He reached his horse, untied him and climbed to the saddle. He headed west along the road.

He was tired and hungry and he was irritable. He was near the end of his patience.

The horse jogged steadily down the road, maintaining a steady, bone-jolting trot that was easy on a horse, but hard on a weary man. Holley let his head drop forward onto his chest. He closed his eyes and dozed, for once oblivious to his surroundings, oblivious to danger that might be waiting ahead of him or pursuing him.

CHAPTER 12

Holley did not arrive in Wild Horse until midnight. All the lights were out except for those in two of the saloons.

He wanted a drink but he didn't want to talk to anyone. Most of all, he wanted to avoid explanations and he knew that, as irritable as he felt, he might lose his head if anyone showed him open hostility or threatened him.

He remembered that Mexico had a bottle in his desk drawer at the jail. He dismounted in front and tied his horse. He could return the animal to the stable later. Right now he wanted that drink and he wanted to see if Lance Custis was all right. He grinned at his own optimism. Hell, what he really wanted to know was whether or not Lance was still in jail.

He opened the door and went inside. He struck a match

74

and lighted the lamp on Mexico's desk. He glanced toward the door leading to the jail cells in the rear. It stood open and he knew he had left it closed. He picked up the lamp and walked back along the corridor. The door of the cell in which Lance had been stood ajar. Lance was gone.

The fact that he was came as no great surprise to Holley. He would have been more surprised to find Lance still in jail.

He returned to the office and put the lamp down on the sheriff's desk. He found the bottle in the bottom drawer. He poured a glass half full and gulped it down. He leaned back in the sheriff's swivel chair and closed his eyes.

Warmth spread through his stomach. His weariness slowly began to evaporate. He stayed in the chair for about ten minutes. Then he went out and led his horse to the stable, where he put him in a stall and gave him some hay and a can of oats.

He returned to the jail. Lance wasn't likely to be going anywhere. He could be picked up later when the judge arrived.

But once more that strange premonition came to him, the certainty that Lance Custis would never go to trial. He shook his head irritably. He was letting the lawlessness of the people in this community get to him. Lance would go to trial and he'd be convicted. But Holley couldn't make himself believe that any more than he believed Jed's killer would be tried and convicted for *his* crime.

He was hungry now and since there was no longer any reason for him to remain at the jail, he blew out the lamp, went outside and crossed the street to the Wild Horse Saloon. He doubted if he could get anything hot to eat, but the free lunch would dull the edge of his hunger enough to let him sleep.

The saloon was nearly deserted. Only Kellison and Seroco were at the bar. They turned their heads and scowled at him.

He ordered beer and laid down a nickel to pay for it. He filled a plate at the end of the bar, then carried plate and beer to a table by the wall. He began to eat.

Kellison and Seroco made several pointed remarks

directed at him. Holley felt his irritability rising, but, conscious of the fact that he was unarmed, he suppressed it determinedly. He finished the free lunch plate, drained his beer glass and got to his feet. He went out without looking at either Seroco or Kellison. He couldn't help wondering where Lance Custis was. If Seroco and Kellison had broken him out of jail, why wasn't he with them?

He walked slowly back to the jail. He went in and locked the door. Without lighting the lamp, he lay down on the office couch. He was almost instantly asleep.

It was light when he awoke. Sunlight streamed in through the office windows. Burt Mexico was standing in the door.

The sheriff looked very tired. He asked, "Lance all right?"

"He's gone. He was gone when I got back."

"Then you must have been the one that helped me out."

"Uh huh. I saw them leave town following you and I figured they might try stopping you."

Mexico grinned. "They're still several miles from town. Walking." The grin faded. "I don't know what the hell I thought was funny about that. When Ben Custis gets as mad as he is right now, he's as dangerous as a grizzly bear."

"When will the judge be here? I thought you were going to bring him back with you."

"He was delayed. He hadn't arrived in Fairplay yet. But I left word that he was to come right away. And I telegraphed Denver for a U. S. marshal to help keep order at the trial."

"Do you think a jury picked from the people here will ever convict Lance?"

Mexico shook his head. "No. But I do know that if we don't bring Lance to trial, we'd just as well fold up and leave and forget about the law."

Holley walked across the room and dumped water into a pan. He washed his face and stared at himself in the mirror on the wall. He had a growth of whiskers on his face. His eyes were red. He said, "Everybody's been run off but the

76

Nordlanders. Do you mind if I ride out there and see if they're all right?"

"Go ahead. Take a rifle with you."

Holley nodded. He picked up the rifle he had used yesterday and got a pocketful of shells for it out of the drawer of the desk. He crammed his hat down on his head and went out into the morning sun, squinting against it in spite of himself.

He went to the stable first and hired a fresh horse. Leading the animal, he went to the restaurant. He ordered ham, eggs, flapjacks and coffee and ate ravenously when his breakfast came. Afterward, he went to the hotel, climbed the stairs, shaved and changed his shirt. It felt strange pinning the deputy badge to his shirt and he wondered wryly how long he would be wearing it. He hadn't come here to help the sheriff enforce the law. He'd come to find Jed's killer but he was beginning to wonder if he would ever succeed in doing so. Jed could have been killed by any one of twenty or more different men.

He went back downstairs, mounted and rode out of town, increasingly uneasy about the safety of the Nordlanders. Frowning, he tried to put a finger on the reason for his sudden uneasiness.

He knew almost immediately. Only the Nordlanders remained to prove it was possible to homestead on Shavano Creek. And as long as they did remain they were an open invitation to other homesteaders to settle there.

Jed had been eliminated and his cabin burned. The other homtsteader family had fled in fear. The ranchers probably didn't figure Holley was going to stay, or else they had already marked him for death. But the Nordlanders were something else. They were a man, a wife and two small children, a family. They had built more permanently than anyone else, so far at least. They had done more to improve their land.

He kicked his horse's sides, promising himself that when he returned to town he was going to get some spurs. All the horses in this Godforsaken country refused to work unless their rider had spurs on his heels.

77

The horse trotted, and finally broke into a reluctant lope. Holley's rump and the insides of his thighs were excruciatingly sore from all the saddle riding he had done in the last couple of days, but he stubbornly held the horse to the loping gait.

He caught himself watching the distant reaches of the valley ahead of him for a plume of smoke. He saw nothing, but half a mile from the Nordlanders' place he suddenly heard the distant sound of a rifle shot. He pulled his horse to a halt in time to catch its echo off the high rocks on the north side of the valley. And now that his horse's hoofs were silent, he caught other sounds, the weaker popping of revolvers, once the deep boom of a shotgun, answering.

He thought of Gerda Nordlander, and of her two small children. They were inside that house, whose flimsy walls wouldn't even stop a revolver bullet. He kicked his horse's sides savagely and kept on kicking until the animal broke into a run. In this way he thundered along the road until the Nordlander house came into sight.

Even at this distance he could see a man behind a corner of the barn. Occasionally the man would poke his gun around the corner and fire at the house. Each time he did, a blue puff of powdersmoke drifted away on the breeze.

There was another man lying prone on the creek bank, a rifle poked out in front of him. Every time he fired, the rifle's roar reverberated from the rocks overlooking the valley on the north. A third man was hidden in the doorway of the root cellar, and his revolver shots sounded like echoes of the rifle shots, coming as they did immediately after them.

Holley's horse pounded into the yard heading straight toward the house. He hoped Lars Nordlander would recognize him and not shoot at him. He could hear the guns of the three besiegers roaring and wondered if one of them would manage to hit him before he got inside.

The door of the house opened and Holley left his saddle and plunged straight toward it. A bullet struck his horse as he reached the door, sounding almost like the violent slap of a hand. The horse wheezed and went to his knees.

Inside, Holley slammed the door violently behind him.

78

He turned immediately toward the nearest window.

Lars Nordlander stood at one side of it, the shotgun Holley had heard gripped in his hands. He turned his head and glanced at Holley. Broken glass littered the floor. Holley asked breathlessly, "How long has this been going on?"

"Couple of hours."

"Any of you hurt?"

Nordlander shook his head. "I don't think they've been seriously trying to hit any of us. They've been breaking the windows. After the windows were broken, they began shooting high at the house itself. They seem to be more interested in scaring us than in killing us."

"Is that shotgun the only gun you have?"

Nordlander nodded.

Holley glanced around the room. Gerda was on the other side of the door with her children. The children were whimpering and their faces were streaked with tears. They lay prone on the floor. Gerda's body between them and the wall of the house provided a shield for them in case any bullets came through the wall.

Holley asked, "What do you think they're going to do when they get tired of shooting at the house?"

"They'll burn the barn and the other outbuildings. They'll probably try to burn the house."

"Do you know any of them?"

"The one with the rifle is Kellison. Seroco is another. I think the third is Lance Custis."

"Do you want to try driving them away?"

Nordlander nodded. "I have been trying but they're not very much afraid of the birdshot in my gun."

Holley edged close to the window and poked the muzzle of the rifle out. He sighted carefully on the corner of the barn and waited. Several moments passed. At last he saw the man poke his head around the corner. He recognized Seroco and fired.

The bullet gouged the barn wall beside Seroco's head, showering him with splinters. He pulled back hastily and did not appear again.

Holley had been watching for the man on the creek

bank, Kellison, to raise his head. Kellison did, firing instantly. Holley swung his gun and fired at the puff of powder-smoke. He missed, but he saw the dirt kick up from the bullet's impact and he heard the slug whine angrily away.

In the doorway of the root cellar, Lance Custis fired now. And Seroco chose that exact instant to break from the corner of the barn and run across the yard.

Nordlander's shotgun roared. Birdshot kicked up puffs of dirt all around Seroco. Some of the shot apparently hit him because he yelled. He turned and raised his revolver, steadying it. His face was twisted and Holley realized that he was taking deliberate aim on Nordlander.

Seroco fired. Holley's gun boomed like an echo and he saw Seroco driven back to fall crumpled in the dust.

He jerked his head around. Nordlander's face was twisted. The shotgun clattered to the floor.

From the far side of the door, Gerda suddenly screamed. The two children began to sob anew. Gerda got up and ran toward Lars, but Holley pushed her roughly down.

He caught Nordlander as he fell, surprised at the man's weight. He carried him through a door on the far side of the room and laid him on a bed. Turning his head, he said, "Come on in here but stay low. I'll see if I can get the children without exposing them."

He hurried back to where the children were. They were screaming now with fear. He gathered them up in his arms. Holding them against his chest, he carried them into the bedroom where their mother was. He put them down almost roughly and ran back into the kitchen, not missing the red stain of Nordlander's blood on the floor, trailing across it toward the bedroom door.

His face was white with anger now. He felt no regret over having killed Seroco out there in the yard. He would now do his best to kill Kellison and Lance Custis too.

But they had lost their enthusiasm for the fight. Their two horses were thundering up the lane toward the road, raising a cloud of dust behind. Seroco lay in the yard on his back, staring up at the blue and cloudless sky.

CHAPTER 13

Holley turned and hurried into the bedroom where Lars Nordlander lay on the bed. Lars' face was gray and his eyes were narrowed with pain. Gerda had his shirt open and was holding a compress against the wound. Her eyes, when they looked up at Holley, were filled with terror.

Holley said, "I'll ride to town for the doctor."

"What about. . . ?"

"Kellison and Lance Custis have gone. Seroco is dead. You'll be all right until I get back. I'll go as fast as I can."

She nodded dazedly. Holley stared at her a moment more, hating to leave her alone, but knowing there was no other way. Bleeding as he was, Lars Nordlander could not be moved.

Holley hurried from the room. He pulled the saddle off his dead horse as quickly as he could and removed the bridle too. He ran to the Nordlander barn, sighing with relief when he found a horse inside. The animal was a big one, probably used as much for work as for riding, but he was all there was.

Holley saddled quickly. He mounted and rode out, using the ends of the reins to whip the horse on, drumming with his heels. The horse broke into a lumbering lope.

Each mile seemed to consume an eternity, nor was Holley's impatience helped by a growing certainty that Lars Nordlander was mortally wounded and would be dead by the time he could bring the doctor back.

Occasionally the big horse tried to slow his gait to a lumbering trot but Holley would not permit it. And finally, more than an hour after leaving the Nordlander homestead, he rode into town.

He found the doctor in his office and blurted what had happened hastily. The doctor snatched his bag, ran down the stairs and headed for the livery barn to get his buggy. Holley shouted after him, "I'll catch you on the road!"

He led the big horse to the jail and tied the reins to the rail. He stepped into the sheriff's office, startled to find Kellison and Ben Custis and Mark already there. Kellison turned his head and said accusingly, "There he is, Burt. I want him arrested for killing Elias Seroco."

Holley crossed the room furiously. He grabbed a handful of Kellison's shirt front and yanked his face close. "You son-of-a-bitch! Tell him where you and Seroco were when he was killed! Tell him Seroco had just shot Lars Nordlander and that Nordlander will probably die. Then you get out of here before I forget myself."

Mexico asked, "Is that right, Jesse?"

Kellison's face flushed uneasily.

Holley raged, "And tell him that Lance Custis was with you when you attacked the Nordlander place. Tell him you and Lance and Seroco had shot out every window in the house and kept the Nordlanders pinned down for more than two hours before I arrived."

Mexico's face was getting red. His voice was dangerously quiet. "Did you and Elias break Lance out of jail?"

"Break him out? What do you mean, break him out? You left him locked up and rode off to Fairplay. The jail was open and anyone could have come in and shot him down. What would have kept Al Slonicker's friends from doing just that, I'd like to know. Sure we turned him loose. We'd do the same thing again."

Mexico got up and crossed the room. He dug his gun savagely into Jesse Kellison's ribs. "Get back there in Lance's cell."

"What the hell's the charge?" Kellison looked appealingly at Ben Custis on the far side of the room.

"Breaking jail will do for a start. Assault with a deadly weapon will back that up. And if Nordlander dies, the

82

charge will be murder in the first degree." Mexico glared at Ben. "Go ahead, Ben. Try getting him away from me. But all you'll get is a body. I give you my solemn word."

For a long, long moment nobody moved. Even their breathing seemed to have stopped. The blood drained out of Jess Kellison's face. He drew a long, shuddering breath and said, "Don't do anything, Ben. He means what he says."

Ben Custis stood there uncertainly a moment. Then, shrugging, he went out the door, followed by his brother Mark.

Holley released Kellison and shoved him away so violently that the man almost fell. Mexico said, "Move Jess," in a voice filled with angry disgust. Kellison slouched back along the corridor and into one of the cells. Burt Mexico slammed and locked the door. He returned to the office, closing the door behind him. Wearily he said, "Well, if Nordlander dies, they've won."

"What do you mean, won?" Holley said angrily. "Mrs. Nordlander and the two kids are still up there. And I'm still here to finish proving up on Jed's homestead claim."

"Mrs. Nordlander can't prove up on that place. She's a woman and she has two little kids. And it's open season on you just like it is on me. I don't think either you or me is going to live out the week."

Holley stared at him. "You think it's that bad?"

Mexico nodded. "Lawlessness is like a contagious disease. You've seen the way it's spread just since you've been here."

"If you think they're going to kill you, why don't you get out?"

"Because it's my job to stay. The oath I took didn't say I'd uphold the law as long as it was easy and safe."

Holley stared at him a moment. "I'm going back up to Nordlander's."

The sheriff nodded. He seemed to have lost interest in Holley. He was staring straight ahead. There was a kind of hopelessness in his eyes that made Holley feel cold inside.

He went out into the sun-washed street. Anger was rising in him, growing like a fire in dry grass. And while he knew

83

his anger could kill him, he didn't try to beat it down. It was high time somebody got angry at the things that were happening. Jed and Slonicker were dead. Nordlander would probably die. And he somehow had the feeling these three deaths were only the beginning. This violence was like a forest fire, devouring everything in its path. It wasn't going to stop.

He dragged the big horse to the stable, glad that the stableman wasn't there. Doc had already left. He got a fresh horse from one of the stalls and changed saddles. Leading the big horse, he rode on out and headed west up the Shavano Creek road.

He could see the dust raised by the doctor's buggy wheels ahead, but in spite of all he could do, he didn't overtake the buggy until it had almost reached Nordlander's lane. Even then he didn't try to talk to Doc. He just fell in behind.

He knew Nordlander was dead when he saw Gerda. She was sitting on the back steps, her face buried in her arms. The two children were playing in the dust in front of her, their faces tear-streaked and frightened. Seroco's body still lay where he had fallen halfway across the yard.

Gerda turned her face toward the doctor. He didn't speak, but went past her into the house, carrying his bag.

Holley dismounted and stood looking down at her. "I'm sorry. When . . . ?"

"Not long after you left. There seemed to be nothing I could do. I tried to stop the bleeding, but I guess he had already lost too much." She began to weep softly.

Holley stared down at her helplessly. He wanted to comfort her but he felt too awkward about it to try. He said lamely, "What can I do?"

Without looking up, she said, "He wanted to be buried here on this land. Would you . . . ?"

"Dig the grave? Of course I will. Where do you want it?"

"I don't know. Just pick out a pretty place."

"All right." He hesitated a moment, then walked to the barn. He found a shovel. There were three willow trees near the creek and that looked like a good place to him. He began the grave in the center of the triangle formed by the

84

three trees. He had scarcely begun when he saw the doctor's buggy go up the lane to the road and head toward town.

He worked slowly but steadily. The ground was hard on top, but after he had dug down about a foot it became softer. He was down four feet when he heard a twig snap and looked up. Gerda Nordlander and her two children were there. Gerda had some cold fried chicken and milk.

He climbed out, washed his hands in the creek, then accepted the food from her. All traces of tears were gone from the children's faces now, but they were still solemn and subdued.

Gerda said, "He was a good man. The children loved him and so did I."

Holley heard iron tires on the road and glanced around. A wagon was creaking down the lane to the Nordlanders' yard. It stopped beside Seroco's body and two men got down and loaded the body in the back. They covered it with a blanket, then turned the wagon around and drove back toward town.

Holley asked, "What will you do now?"

"We will stay here. This is our home."

"How can you . . . ?"

"Farm it by ourselves? I don't know, but we will somehow."

He didn't think there was much chance that they could, but he didn't say anything. Gerda Nordlander would find out soon enough that the harassment wasn't going to stop just because Lars Nordlander was dead. He finished eating and returned to his work. Gerda took the children and went back to the house.

It was about mid-afternoon when he finished the grave. He left the shovel at the graveside and returned to the barn. He found a saw, a hammer, some nails. By hunting around diligently, he found enough boards to build a coffin. He was a fair carpenter and by sundown, the coffin was finished. He walked up to the house.

Gerda was feeding the children. Holley knocked and went in when she called to him. He said, "I made a coffin for him. Do you want to bury him tonight or wait until morning?"

85

"I'd rather wait until morning. Would you mind going to town for the preacher?"

He shook his head. "Will you be all right?"

"I'm not afraid."

He doubted if there would be any more trouble right away, and he didn't want to start tongues wagging by staying overnight. He said, "I'll be going then. I'll be back with the preacher first thing in the morning."

"Thank you." She seemed listless, almost beaten. Again he wanted to comfort her without knowing how. He hesitated a moment, then stepped out into the gathering dusk.

He found his horse, mounted and rode up the lane. Where it joined the road, he stopped and looked back. Gerda had lighted a lamp in the kitchen. It made a dim square of light where the open doorway was.

Holley rode toward town. He was aware that he was becoming ever more deeply involved with this community. And he still didn't know who Jed's killer was.

Riding, he couldn't stop his thoughts from returning to Gerda Nordlander and to her two little children. She couldn't stay out there. It all boiled down to that. Men who would shoot indiscriminately into a flimsy frame house where they knew a woman and two children were wouldn't hesitate to harass her by cutting fences, by burning buildings, even by burning the house in which she lived.

His farm in Illinois suddenly seemed remote, almost unreal to him. Strangely enough, for the first time since leaving it he was not anxious to return.

He passed the lane leading to what was left of Jed's homestead and stopped his horse there momentarily. In the starlight, he looked across the fields that Jed had fenced.

He knew how Gerda felt about leaving because he suddenly felt the same way himself. His brother Jed's lifeblood was here, forever a part of this piece of contested land.

He might be forced to leave, Holley thought, or he might be killed like Jed had been. Gerda might also be forced to leave. But damn them, they were going to get a fight. He

86

wasn't going to leave like a whipped pup, with his tail between his legs.

He kicked the horse into motion and clattered down the road. It was late when he came into Wild Horse. Since he had no idea how to find the preacher, or even where the church was, he went to the jail to ask Burt Mexico.

The sheriff was asleep, but he came up from the office couch like a cat when Holley opened the door. Holley said, "It's me. Nordlander is dead."

"I know. Doc told me."

"Mrs. Nordlander asked me to bring the preacher for the burying."

"His name is Isaac Morris. Come on. I'll show you where he lives."

He put on his boots and Holley followed him out into the night. There were only a few lights in town. Holley got the strangest feeling that they were being watched, even though he knew it was impossible.

CHAPTER 14

Isaac Morris was a bearded man with piercing blue eyes and a tall, gaunt frame on which his nightshirt hung like a sack. He promised to be out at the Nordlander place at dawn.

Holley walked back to the jail with Burt Mexico. He asked, "Any idea where Lance Custis is?"

"He's probably at the ranch. I don't figure there's any sense in picking him up until we're ready for him, and besides, I wouldn't mind having a U. S. marshal to back us up."

They reached the jail and went inside. There was a fire in the office stove and a pot of coffee simmering on top of it. Holley walked over and poured himself a cup.

Mexico said unexpectedly, "Sam Rankin is dead. He died this afternoon."

"Who . . . ?"

"Rankin was the one you jabbed in the belly with the pitchfork down at the livery stable."

"How's the other one, Trimmer?"

"Doc says not good. He may lose his leg."

Holley felt sick at his stomach. He had now killed two men since coming here, Rankin and Seroco. Another was in danger of losing a leg because of him. Yet none of the trouble had been of his own making, neither the fight at the livery barn nor the trouble at the Nordlander place.

He said, "I was going to stay in town until morning but I've changed my mind. I'm going back up to the Nordlander place."

"Better not. Gerda Nordlander can get along without any gossip now."

"I figured on staying out of sight. She won't know I'm there and neither will anybody else."

The sheriff shrugged. "Go ahead. I guess if any trouble starts it will be out there."

Holley went out. Even the saloons were dark. He untied his horse, mounted and rode out of town, the rifle resting in the crook of his right arm. He had felt as though he was being watched a while ago. He felt the same way now and he wondered what they were waiting for. Why didn't they kill him, from ambush, and have it over with?

Gerda and her children would have to leave if they burned her house. If they also killed him, then nothing would stand in their way. Lance Custis certainly wasn't going to be convicted of killing Slonicker. Neither would he be convicted of complicity in the death of Lars Nordlander.

The horse trotted steadily. The gait was so rough that Holley drew back on the reins until the horse slowed to a walk. He doubted if there was any hurry about getting back to the Nordlander place. He doubted if the ranchers would bother Gerda and her children tonight. They'd wait until Gerda took the children and went to town for supplies.

The house was dark when he arrived. He dismounted and led the horse to a spot a hundred yards away from which he could watch. He sat down and put his back against a tree. He found a cigar and lighted it.

He finished the cigar and threw it away. He dozed intermittently. At last he saw gray beginning to gather above the eastern horizon. Not long afterward the minister, Isaac Morris, drove his buggy down the lane into the yard.

Holley waited until he had gone into the house. Then he got up, mounted and rode in after him. He tied his horse, went to the door and knocked.

The children were still asleep but Gerda was up, starting a fire in the stove. She cooked breakfast for Holley and for the preacher. Then she awakened the children and fed them and herself.

When they had finished, and while Gerda washed and dressed the children for the funeral, Holley and Isaac Morris carried the coffin in and put Lars Nordlander's body into it. They carried it out again.

Holley hitched the team to the wagon and drove it to the house. He and the preacher loaded the coffin into it. Gerda and the children mounted to the seat. The preacher drove and Holley walked behind.

At the graveside they unloaded the coffin. Holley tied ropes to it so that it could be lowered into the grave.

Isaac Morris opened his Bible. His voice was harsh as he read the passages. He finished with, "The Lord giveth and the Lord taketh away. Blessed be the name of the Lord."

He closed the book and nodded at Holley. Together they lowered the coffin into the grave. Stooping, the preacher picked up a handful of earth which he let sift through his fingers into the grave.

Gerda and her children were weeping. Holley helped them up to the wagon seat, the children first, Gerda last. The preacher drove back to the house with them. Holley stayed to fill in the grave.

By the time he had finished, the sun was well up into the

sky. He walked to the house, put the wagon away behind the barn. He dragged the dead horse away from the house, then unhitched the horses and turned them into the corral.

The preacher and Gerda came out the door. The preacher shook her hand, then climbed to his buggy seat and drove away.

The children were playing behind the house. Gerda looked at Holley, her eyes brimming with unshed tears. "I feel so alone."

He nodded. "I know."

"Are you going to stay here? Or will you be going home?"

"Three days ago I'd have said I was going home. Now I don't know. Maybe I will stay. It seems like I owe that much to Jed." He studied her face a moment. Her eyes were red from weeping and her face was pale. "You can't farm this place alone, you know. Besides, they'll burn you out the first time you leave and go to town."

"Then I won't go to town."

"That won't stop them. As long as you stay, you're an invitation to other homesteaders."

She smiled faintly. "Maybe some of them will accept the invitation and settle here." She studied him a moment. "Tell me about yourself, and about Jed."

He shrugged. "There's not much to tell. We grew up in Illinois. I enlisted in the northern army during the war but I never got into the fighting. Jed stayed home and helped run the farm. Both my father and mother died of typhoid before I could get home. When I did get back . . ." He smiled ruefully. "Jed and I had different ideas about how the farm should be run. I guess if I had given him a chance to try out some of his ideas, he wouldn't have gone away."

She shook her head. "He'd have gone away. He was the age when boys leave home. He wanted to do something on his own."

"Did you know him very well?"

"Not very well. He used to come here and talk to Lars. He used to go to the Hennies homestead sometimes to talk to Pete."

90

"Have you any ideas on who might have killed him?"

She shook her head again. "Nothing definite enough to put into words. You know who stood to benefit if he was driven away. Both Al Slonicker and the Custis brothers wanted the land he claimed."

The children had left their play. They now stood about ten feet away, staring at Holley solemnly. He smiled at them, but they did not return the smile. He began to feel uncomfortable and was no less so when he discovered that Gerda's eyes were twinkling. She said, "You haven't been around children very much, have you?"

He shook his head.

"They like you."

"How can you tell that?"

"I know them." Speaking to the children she said, "This is Mr. Holley, children. Come and say hello to him."

They approached so warily that Holley had to smile. But it was a warm, friendly smile and it broke the ice. They came and stood close to him and he knelt and put an arm around each of them. Gerda said, "Their names are Danny and Sue. Danny is four and Sue is five."

Holley said suddenly, "I ought to go back to town. If the judge has arrived, the sheriff will be needing me."

"I noticed the deputy's badge."

He didn't want to leave. There was suddenly a closeness between the four of them, a closeness he wished would never go away.

But he couldn't stay. He had already stayed too long. He knew how eagerly the gossips would seize upon his presence here. Gerda was young. Her husband had been almost old enough to be her grandfather and he now was dead. That was a situation made to order for gossiping tongues.

He could tell that she understood his thoughts. He got up awkwardly. Their glances locked briefly. It was Gerda who looked away.

He said, "I'll come back every day. Is there anything you need?"

91

She shook her head.

Holley looked at the two children. They were both staring up solemnly at him. He said, "Good-bye Danny. Good-bye, Sue."

"Bye." He realized suddenly how little he had heard their voices and how much terror they had seen in the last few days. He wondered how much more lay ahead. He asked suddenly, "Do you have to stay?"

She nodded. "This place was Lars' way of giving me the security his age would not otherwise allow him to provide. But he expected to live until Danny was old enough to help. He thought that then we would be all right. I can't leave because if I do it will mean he gave his life for nothing."

Holley said, "I shouldn't have asked."

Gerda smiled. "It's all right. Thank you for worrying about me. I doubt if they'll do anything worse than burn us out. I don't think they'll harm any of us."

"And if they burn you out?"

"We'll cross that bridge when we come to it."

He mounted his horse. The three of them stood at the kitchen door and watched him ride away. A breeze stirred Gerda's dress and hair. The little girl, Sue, raised her hand and waved.

Holley waved back, his throat unaccountably feeling tight. He kicked the horse into a steady trot, wishing he had asked Gerda to bring the children and come with him. He knew suddenly that he wanted her. He wanted to marry her and raise the two children as his own.

But he realized that she would have refused. Regardless of the pressures on her, it was too soon after Lars Nordlander's death.

For Holley, there was no longer any doubt about whether he would stay or not. He couldn't leave as long as Gerda and her two children remained.

He forced the horse into a steady lope. He hoped the judge was already in Wild Horse. He hoped the trial could begin tomorrow, because he sensed that the trial of Lance Custis would bring the slumbering violence that threatened the country to a head.

A mile short of town, he met Burt Mexico. The sheriff was holding his horse to a steady trot. He stopped when he reached Holley. "I was coming after you. The judge is in town and we have to pick up Lance Custis."

"What about the marshal? Didn't he show up?"

Mexico shook his head. "Not yet. Maybe he'll be on hand tomorrow for the start of the trial."

"You think we can take Lance?"

Mexico grinned doubtfully. "We can try. Unless you want to back out. I won't blame you if you do."

Holley said, "I'm not thinking about backing out. I'm just wondering why they should resist giving Lance up if they know he's going to be acquitted."

"Whether he's convicted or not isn't what worries them. What they really want to do is discredit the law. If they can drive the law out of the country, then no homesteader will dare to stay."

Holley nodded. "All right. Let's go."

The two rode upcountry toward the Custis ranch. Burt Mexico's face lacked its usual ruddiness. Holley wondered if his own face was as pale.

CHAPTER 15

Holley and Burt Mexico had taken Lance Custis out from under the noses of his three brothers once before, but Holley had the uneasy conviction it wasn't going to be as easy this time. Not that it had been particularly easy the other time.

He wondered whether all four of the Custis brothers were at home. He hadn't seen any of them since yesterday when the sheriff had arrested Kellison, so he supposed they were. Thinking of the Custis brothers, he asked, "Do you think Kellison will still be in jail when you get back?"

Mexico grinned wryly. "Hell, I don't know. I'm not real sure of anything anymore."

"Have you got a plan for taking Lance?"

Mexico shook his head, and Holley stared at him. Mexico was like a man forcing himself to function but unable to think clearly or plan ahead. He would try to take Lance because it was his duty, but he had no hope of bringing it off and firmly believed he was going to be killed. Holley said, "Wait a minute."

Mexico halted his horse. Holley said, "Maybe you're willing to barge in there and get yourself killed trying to do something you think is impossible, but I'm not. If I go in there and risk my neck, I want it to be for something I think is going to work."

"You can't make the impossible possible."

"We took Lance once before. There's no reason why we can't do the same thing again."

"Except that they'll be ready for us this time."

"Then we'll have to create a diversion."

"What do you mean by that?"

"Well, they're pretty good at burning things. I don't see why we can't do it too."

"I'm not going to enforce the law by breaking it."

"Why not? What's the alternative? If you let them kill you there won't be any law. Is that what you want?"

"No." Mexico straightened in his saddle. "All right. Maybe we can pull it off."

Holley said, "I noticed part of a haystack between the house and the creek. It ought to be dry enough to burn."

They were passing Al Slonicker's land, approaching the corner of the Custis place. Already Holley could see the top two stories of the three-story log house. He said, "I'll go down in the creek bottom and work my way up toward the house. Don't do anything until you see the smoke."

"Maybe they'll guess it's a trick."

"Maybe. Have you got a better idea?"

Mexico shook his head. Holley said, "I'll try to hide near
94

enough to the haystack so I can get the drop on them when they come to fight the fire."

He headed for the creek along a narrow strip of unclaimed land that lay between Slonicker's and the Custis place. He reached the creek and looked back. Mexico was working his way cautiously closer, staying in the ditch that ran along one side of the road.

Now Holley hurried, sometimes riding in the water to avoid heavy brush, sometimes leaving it. The huge house loomed above the trees and brush and was visible to him most of the time.

Immediately below it, he tied his horse and went on afoot. He still had the rifle and as he slipped through the heavy brush, he checked its loads.

He kept the partially used haystack between himself and the house. Reaching it, he poked his head around its corner and stared toward the house. A few chickens were scratching around the door and half a dozen weaner pigs were rooting in mud created by dishwater thrown out the door. But he saw none of the Custis brothers.

He found a match and struck it on the buttplate of the gun. He tossed it up onto the haystack. The hay flared almost as swiftly as had the hay in Slonicker's barn.

He retreated quickly and concealed himself in brush, working to one side a little so that he could see both the flaming haystack and the house.

In the lane beyond the house he glimpsed Burt Mexico working his way down the fence at one side of it, leading his horse. The sheriff was partially concealed by weeds that grew along the fence, but Holley knew that if he could see Mexico, so could those in the house.

Still, some chances had to be taken and it wasn't probable that any of the Custis brothers would be looking up the lane. Their attention would be on the burning stack.

A breeze, blowing from creek to house, carried a heavy pall of smoke across the yard. Suddenly Holley heard a shout.

The back door slammed. Several men were shouting now. He heard the clang of buckets on the porch. He saw Ben Custis running toward the creek, a bucket in each

95

hand. The second man, immediately behind him, was Mark. The third was Lance and behind Lance came Ralph.

He wished Lance could have been last because that would have given Mexico a chance to capture him easily. But at least all four of the brothers had buckets in their hands. They had neither rifles nor shotguns but only the revolvers they wore.

Mexico was now running openly across the yard. Holley heard him shout and saw Ralph turn his head.

He stepped out of the concealing brush and strode swiftly toward Ben. Ben dropped the two buckets he was carrying. His hand started toward his gun.

Holley brought the rifle to his shoulder, sighting it. He yelled, "Don't do it! I'll kill you if you do!"

Ben stopped, frozen where he stood. Mark still held the two buckets he had been carrying but he had also stopped. So had Lance. Ralph was beyond Holley's line of vision but he figured Mexico would take care of him. Holley called, "Easy now, Ben. Unbuckle the gunbelt and let it drop. Mark, don't you move. Don't you move either, Lance, until I tell you what to do."

Ben let his gunbelt fall. His face was livid with fury. Holley called, "Now take two or three steps away from it. Back toward Mark."

Ben obeyed. Holley said, "You're next, Mark. Unbuckle it and let it drop."

Mark did. Holley said, "Now the two of you back up toward Lance."

He could now see Ralph beyond Lance. Mexico stood near him. He had Ralph's gun and belt in his hand. He had his revolver in his other hand. Mexico said, "You're last, Lance. Let it drop."

For a moment it looked as though Lance might make a fight of it, but he changed his mind. Mexico said, "Gather up those three guns, Holley, and go get your horse."

Holley did. When he came back, Mexico took the guns from him. "Lance, get up on Holley's horse."

Lance mounted while the sheriff held the reins. Mexico said, "Get up behind him, Holley."

Holley mounted behind Lance. Mexico said, "Take him

to town and put him in jail. I'll hold these boys here long enough for you to get a start."

Holley drummed on his horse's ribs with his heels. Lance's hands hung at his sides, his left one close to the barrel of Holley's rifle. Holley said, "Put 'em on the saddle horn and keep them there unless you want a big knot on the side of your head."

Lance obeyed. Holley realized how tight and nervous his voice had been and grinned faintly to himself. He'd convinced Lance he meant what he said, anyway.

He glanced behind when they reached the road. Mexico still held the three brothers where they had been earlier. He had a moment's worry about the sheriff's safety, but then he decided there would be small reason for the Custis brothers to kill him now.

He was almost halfway to town when he heard the steady drum of galloping hoofs. He turned his head, relieved to see Burt Mexico coming. Half a mile behind Burt he could see the horses of the three Custis brothers, but they did not seem to be trying to close the gap between the sheriff and themselves. Mexico grinned as he rode up to Holley. "I'm beginning to think I've got nine lives. I didn't think we were going to pull that off."

Lance sneered, "It won't do you any good. There ain't a jury in the country that will find me guilty."

Holley looked at him. "What about Slonicker's friends?"

"He ain't got no friends."

"He was doing your dirty work when he burned my brother's shack."

"He was like hell. He wanted that place for himself."

Holley didn't pursue the subject any further. They reached town, went immediately to the jail, dismounted and went inside. Holley was mildly surprised to find that Kellison was still in his cell.

Mexico left immediately. "I'm going over to the hotel and see if the judge has arrived. Don't let Lance's brothers in."

Mexico hadn't been gone more than a few minutes when Holley saw the Custis brothers ride into town. They did not come to the jail, but instead tied their horses to the rail in

97

front of the Wild Horse Saloon. They went inside.

The sheriff was back within fifteen minutes. He said, "The judge is over at the hotel. He says he'll try both Kellison and Lance tomorrow if I can get a jury together by that time." He rummaged through the top drawer of his desk. "I've got a list here someplace." He drew out a paper on which thirty or forty names were written. "Here's the panel. I'll go notify some of them to appear for jury duty tomorrow." He left the office, closing the door behind him. Holley crossed to it and shot the bolt.

He returned to the sheriff's swivel chair and sat down. The rifle was leaning against the desk where he could reach it easily. Out in back, Kellison and Lance Custis were talking, their voices making a steady drone, but he couldn't understand their words.

A sudden, uneasy feeling came over him. Kellison, Lance Custis and Elias Seroco had attacked the Nordlander house and killed Lars Nordlander. Now, with Seroco dead, Kellison and Lance were the only witnesses remaining alive, except for himself and Gerda Nordlander. He thought he knew what they were discussing back there in their cells. They were getting together on a story that they intended to tell in court.

With growing uneasiness he imagined what the story would be. They would say they had ridden to Nordlander's place to offer him their help, to try and smooth over past differences. He had fired on them, pinning them down so that they couldn't get away. In an attempt to make good their escape, they had opened fire on the house, trying to make him stop shooting at them long enough for them to withdraw.

At this point, they would say, Holley had appeared on the scene. They had let him enter the house, without shooting directly at him, only shooting his horse in an effort to frighten him away.

They would probably say he had killed Nordlander himself because he wanted Nordlander's wife. Then he had killed Seroco so he could claim Seroco had killed Nordlander.

An outrageous story, Holley told himself. But was it so

98

outrageous? Would it sound outrageous to the judge? And wouldn't the jurymen, who wanted to be rid of him anyway, seize on the story as a chance to do legally what they would otherwise have to do by violence?

He crossed the room and opened the door leading to the cells. Instantly both Lance Custis and Kellison stopped talking. Holley called sourly, "You two need anything?"

"Nothin' you can give us, Deputy. Is the judge in town?"

"Uh huh. If the sheriff can find enough jurymen, you'll go on trial tomorrow."

"You too, deputy," said Kellison. "When Lance and me tell our stories, you'll be the one on trial."

Holley shut the door and returned to the swivel chair. He had one cigar left, he discovered. He took it out, bit off the end and lighted it. He blew a smoke ring at the ceiling, a frown remaining on his face. He discovered that he was worse scared of a legal frame-up than he was that one of the Custis brothers would try killing him.

What scared him the worst was the uneasy belief that they would be able to make it stick. Gerda would testify for him, of course. But would her word, the word of the young wife of an elderly homesteader, be believed in this country where everyone feared homesteaders and wanted to be rid of them?

Anger began to smolder anew in Holley's mind. He told himself he was being a fool and imagining things. He had no reason to believe incriminating him had been the subject of the conversation between Kellison and Lance.

But from their viewpoint, it made a lot of sense. Furthermore, if Lance was acquitted of killing Slonicker, Holley would immediately become a prime suspect again. He had admitted burning Slonicker's barn. He had been there when Slonicker was killed, or at least he had been nearby. Suddenly Holley felt like an animal caught in a trap.

CHAPTER 16

The trials began promptly at 9:00 A.M. the following day in the Shavano County courthouse, a large log structure at the upper end of Shavano Street three blocks from the jail.

Jury selection consumed almost an hour. The defense attorney challenged three prospective jurors who were known to have been friends of Al Slonicker.

Lance Custis was first on trial, and Sheriff Burt Mexico was the first prosecution witness. He testified that he had tracked Lance's horse from the scene of the crime to the Custis ranch. He said Holley had found the horse in the Custis barn, and that he had identified the animal by his split hoof.

The defense attorney, Lucas Wellman, got up to cross-examine. He asked the sheriff if it was not possible that someone else had used the horse, that someone else had ridden it to the Custis place in an effort to incriminate Lance. Mexico had to admit it was possible and he was excused.

Next, the prosecutor called two friends of Slonicker. Both testified as to the hard feelings that had existed between Slonicker and the Custis family. One had witnessed a quarrel between Slonicker and Ben Custis several months earlier.

The prosecutor rested his case. Wellman called the Custis brothers one after another. All three testified that Lance had been with them constantly on the day Slonicker

100

was killed. The judge instructed the jury and they conferred briefly without leaving the jury box. The foreman got up and announced their verdict. It was that Lance was not guilty.

Judge Myer, frowning, called the case against Kellison. It was as quickly disposed of. When the jury had announced their "not guilty" verdict, the defense attorney rose. "Certain accusations have been made, Your Honor, that it is my duty to report to you. Lance Custis has been tried and found not guilty of the murder of Al Slonicker. Mr. Kellison has been found not guilty of complicity in the death of Lars Nordlander. That leaves the question open, Your Honor, as to who actually did kill both Mr. Slonicker and Mr. Nordlander. My clients, both present when the latter man was killed, say he was killed by Mr. Cole Holley, a newcomer to this country, because he wanted Mr. Nordlander's young wife."

Holley glanced at Gerda Nordlander sitting in the rear of the courtroom with her two children. Her face was flushed, but her eyes defiantly met those of the courtroom spectators who turned their heads.

Judge Myer glanced at the prosecutor. "Mr. Enlow?"

Enlow shrugged. "I'll charge him if Your Honor thinks it proper."

"I do. An accusation has been made. If Mr. Holley is not guilty, he deserves to be cleared. If he is guilty, he should be made to pay the penalty."

Holley was asked to come forward and was seated in the prisoner's box with Sheriff Mexico. He was asked if he wanted a jury and he shook his head, preferring that the question of his guilt or innocence be decided by the judge, who was impartial, rather than by a jury composed of men who bitterly resented the intrusion of homesteaders.

He conferred briefly with Frank Delehanty, a young lawyer who agreed to defend him. The prosecutor called Jess Kellison and Kellison told the story he and Lance Custis had evidently cooked up between themselves and carefully rehearsed. Lance was next on the stand and he corroborated Kellison's story. Both men swore Holley had spent the night with Gerda at Nordlander's place the night

101

after he was killed. Both men swore they had seen Holley shoot Seroco and that they had heard a shot inside the house immediately afterward, the shot that killed Nordlander. They hadn't seen it fired, they said, but it had to have been fired either by Holley or by Gerda Nordlander.

Sheriff Mexico was called next. He admitted Holley had been at the Nordlander house when Lars Nordlander was killed.

The prosecution rested. Holley caught Judge Myer looking at him, a slight frown on his face. The defense attorney called him to the stand.

He told what had happened, simply and straightforwardly. Delehanty called Gerda and she corroborated his story in a frightened but determined voice. While she was testifying, her children cried with fright back at the rear of the courtroom in their seats.

Delehanty called Sheriff Mexico next. The sheriff told of the beating Holley had received the night of his arrival in Wild Horse. He told of the way Holley's brother's shack had been burned. He related some of the background in the case, the murder of Holley's brother Jed, the intimidation of Pete Hennies and his family, the attempted intimidation of the Nordlanders.

The judge called a recess until two o'clock. Mexico touched Holley's arm. "I'd better keep you in custody. Come on down to the jail with me." He grinned. "You'll get a dinner and it won't cost you a dime."

Holley walked to the jail with him. He asked, "What do you think? What's the judge going to say?"

"Not guilty. Judge Myer knows what's going on down here. He's not a fool. He saw through that story Lance and Kellison told about how they happened to be at Nordlander's shooting up the house."

"And if he turns me loose. What then?"

"I don't see what the Custis brothers would have to bellyache about. Lance and Kellison got off too."

But there was no conviction in the sheriff's voice. His eyes were worried and there was a slight frown on his face.

102

His hands trembled as he ate the dinner the restaurant had sent up to the jail.

Holley ate his own dinner, as worried as the sheriff was. Ben Custis and his brothers were crude and unimaginative and they were brutally direct. When someone stood in their way, killing was the answer that immediately suggested itself to them. He was sure now that one of them killed his brother Jed. He was equally sure they would try to kill him if the judge acquitted him. He did not doubt that they would kill Gerda Nordlander if there was no other way of getting rid of her.

At a few minutes before two, Holley and Burt Mexico walked back to the courthouse. It was already full. The spectators rose when the judge came in. He rapped for order, then ordered Holley to stand. When Holley had obeyed, he said, "Cole Holley, this court finds you not guilty of the charge of murder. You are free to go."

For several moments there was complete silence in the room. Ben Custis broke the silence by jumping to his feet. "Why God damn you, Judge, you know he's guilty as hell! You know the son-of-a-bitch killed Nordlander so's he could have that good-lookin' young wife of his."

Judge Myer's face turned pale. His gavel came down furiously. "Silence!" he roared. "Or I'll hold you in contempt!"

"You don't have to hold me in contempt! I ain't got nothin' but contempt for a chicken-livered bastard like you!"

"Sheriff, arrest that man!"

Mexico got to his feet. He turned toward Ben Custis, but Ben had drawn his gun. So had Mark and Ralph. Spectators scrambled to get out of the way.

Mexico turned his head and looked questioningly at the judge. His face was white and his eyes desperate, but Holley realized that he would try taking Ben Custis if the judge ordered it, even though doing so meant certain death.

Judge Myer shook his head. Ben Custis backed toward the door, followed by Mark and Ralph, also backing, also with guns in their hands. Lance was working his way along the side of the room, heading toward the door. Judge Myer said, "Let them go. I don't want to be responsible for bloodshed in this court."

Ben Custis reached the door and disappeared. His brothers followed him. Lance was the last to go. When he had disappeared the courtroom was suddenly filled with confusion as all the spectators began talking excitedly at once.

Gerda Nordlander remained in her seat. The children had stopped crying but their eyes were scared. Judge Myer was frowning and his face was pale. Mexico's hands were shaking violently. A moment ago he had been facing certain death. The letdown was almost too much for him. He sat down and gripped his knees, trying to steady both knees and hands. He looked up at Holley and grinned shakily. "Jesus! I'd just as soon not come that close to the pearly gates again!"

The last of the spectators filed out of the room. Both defense attorneys had also gone, but Dave Enlow, the prosecutor, remained. Judge Myer looked helplessly at Mexico and then at Enlow. "Well, gentlemen?"

Enlow, visibly shaken, said, "You did right to let them go, Judge. Contempt of court isn't worth getting anybody killed over."

"There's more involved here than contempt of court. The law itself is on trial. I believe that in their anger they were capable of killing the sheriff right here in this room. I think afterward they might have killed me, and you too, Mr. Enlow."

"So what do we do now?"

Myer frowned. "Three of them are guilty of assault with a deadly weapon right here in court. Conviction carries a sentence of from one to fifteen years. As things stand, however, I see no point in arresting them and bringing them to trial. Let's wait until I can get a United States marshal in here with some deputies." He stared at the men in the courtroom. "This is the most flagrant defiance of the law I have ever encountered. We ought to be able to handle it by swearing in a posse of citizens, but that isn't possible in this instance because the local people seem to support the Custis brothers' defiance of the law."

"Then what good will a federal marshal do? Even if you arrest the Custis brothers and bring them to trial, no jury chosen from the people hereabouts will convict them of anything."

"I'll try the case in Fairplay."

Enlow said, "You'd better get your U. S. marshal and his deputies in here fast. Four men have been killed in Wild Horse or nearby in less than a week. I would also suggest that you arm yourself."

"You're not seriously suggesting that they might harm me?"

"I'm suggesting exactly that. The Custis brothers didn't have much respect for the law a week ago. They have even less since they have been successful in flaunting it. Lance killed Al Slonicker. Everybody knows he did. Furthermore, he and Kellison were present when Seroco killed Nordlander and that makes them just as guilty as Seroco was."

Judge Myer looked at Burt Mexico. "What do you think, Burt?"

"I'd get a gun if I was you. And I'd stay close to my hotel room. I'll give you all the protection I can, Judge, but I can't be with you all the time."

Judge Myer nodded. "Bring a shotgun to my room, Burt. A double-barrel. I'm used to that kind."

Mexico looked at Holley. "You had better get out of town. Catch the first stage and don't come back until this is settled."

Holley fingered the deputy's star on his shirt. He shook his head stubbornly.

Enlow, Mexico and the judge went out and stood for a moment talking on the courthouse steps. Holley went back to Gerda Nordlander. He smiled at the children but their expressions of fright did not relax. Gerda asked, "What do you think I should do?"

"I don't know. If you stay in town it's a cinch they'll burn you out. If you go home . . . well, it's dangerous."

105

"If that's the choice, I'm going home."

He nodded, knowing it would be useless trying to change her mind. Besides, he wasn't sure that she wouldn't be as safe at home as she would be right here in town. He said, "I'll come up every day."

She nodded. "Thank you." She got up and, taking a child's hand in each of her own, walked to the door.

Holley followed her outside. He helped her into her buckboard and lifted the children up. He watched her drive out of town, smiling a little at the straight way she sat in the buckboard seat, at the way she held her head so high.

He was now almost sure that one of the Custis brothers had killed his brother Jed. Perhaps when the time came for a showdown with them, they would admit doing it. Fearing the law no more than they apparently did, there was no reason for them to lie.

He stared down the street. Little groups of people stood here and there talking excitedly. It was as if the people relished the showdown between the Custis brothers and the law.

Holley walked slowly down to the jail. It was open season on him from this moment on, just as it was on the sheriff and the judge.

Maybe what was needed was a troop of cavalry to maintain order and enforce the law if it turned out that a tough federal marshal and some deputies weren't enough.

Mexico met him at the front door of the jail. "Judge Myer is writing a letter. He wants you to go to Fairplay with it, and if the marshal hasn't arrived there yet, he wants you to mail it to Denver for him." He shook his head. "I've never seen the judge scared before, but he's scared today."

Holley said, "I'll go on over to the hotel and get the letter." He grinned faintly at Mexico. "Mind going down to the stable and getting me a horse? The stableman always gives me a nag, but he just might give you a decent horse."

Mexico headed for the livery barn. Holley walked toward the hotel. He had a hunch that he was being watched. He was almost sure he would be followed when he rode out of town.

CHAPTER 17

The judge was just finishing his letter when Holley arrived. He asked him to sit down while he sealed it and addressed the envelope. "Check the hotel in Fairplay, Mr. Holley, to see if Marshal Ferguson has arrived. If he has not, give this letter to the postmaster personally."

"Do you want me to wait in Fairplay until Ferguson arrives?"

Judge Myer shook his head. "No need for that. Besides, he may not even come through Fairplay. He may come up the Arkansas."

Holley took the envelope. Judge Myer smiled faintly at him. "Don't judge all of our Colorado country by the lawless element here, Mr. Holley."

Holley shook his head. The judge's door closed and Holley heard the key turn in the lock.

He put the letter into his pocket so that it could not be seen and returned to the jail. There was a gray horse tied in front. Mexico came to the door. "That gray is a good horse. I've ridden him myself."

"Thanks." Holley mounted.

"They'll know where you're going and they'll follow you."

Holley nodded. "I figured they would."

Mexico handed up a Spencer repeating rifle and a box of cartridges. "Want a revolver too?"

Holley shook his head. "I'm no good with one."

"Good luck."

"The same to you. That U. S. marshal will be here in a day or two. Don't do anything foolish while you're waiting for him."

Mexico grinned. "Not likely."

Holley headed north out of town, taking the stage road that followed the Arkansas. It was almost four o'clock.

He glanced back once. The sheriff stood in front of the jail looking after him. There were a couple of dozen people on the street but no one seemed to be particularly interested. He saw no horsemen. He saw none of the Custis brothers but he wasn't fool enough to believe that they wouldn't follow him.

Once clear of the town, he touched his heels to the horse's sides and was gratified when the animal broke eagerly into a gallop. He rounded the first bend in the road and pulled off to one side. Working his way carefully back so that he could see the road between himself and town, he waited.

No one appeared. Frowning, Holley reined his horse back into the road and went on. He couldn't believe that no one was following him. They had surely observed him going into the hotel and they must have guessed he had gone to see the judge. They had seen him leaving town and they could scarcely have failed to reach the conclusion that he was going on some errand for the judge, probably to bring reinforcements for the law.

Of one thing Holley was very sure. Ben Custis wasn't going to let those reinforcements arrive if he could help it.

Uneasiness crept through his thoughts. He caught himself pushing his horse faster than he should, and stopped the animal to let him rest. The horse's neck and shoulders were wet with sweat. There was froth on his mouth.

Ahead was the bridge across the Arkansas, the place where the road left the river and began the climb toward Trout Creek Pass. The sun hung low over the mountains to the west. Sundown was not far away.

Suddenly his glance caught a lift of dust back along the road. He stared at it, surprised that he felt relieved. He grinned at his own inconsistency. He'd been afraid of being followed. Now he was relieved to discover that they were following him.

He mounted and went on, pacing the horse more carefully. Occasionally he glanced back, checking the relative position of those pursuing him. He was able to count them because they were closer now. There were five, he supposed the Custis brothers and Kellison. Those five seemed to be the chief troublemakers in the country around Wild Horse, he thought. If they could be eliminated, peace might return to the valley of Shavano Creek.

The sun was just sinking behind the snow-clad peaks of the divide when Holley clattered noisily across the Arkansas bridge. His pursuers had continued to gain ground. They were now no more than a quarter mile behind. As he stared at them they spurred their horses and came on at a run.

Holley kicked his own horse into a run, grateful that Mexico had hired a willing mount for him. He pounded up the steep and rocky road leading to the pass. The pursuit crossed the bridge, the thunder of their horses' hoofs audible to Holley a quarter mile away. Staring back, he saw one of them raise a gun and saw a puff of smoke. He didn't hear the bullet and assumed it had fallen short. But there was no longer any doubt what his pursuers' intentions were. They meant to kill him if they could.

Fortunately, it would soon be dark. All he had to do was stay ahead until it was.

The sun went down and the grays of dusk crept across the land. The sky grew ever darker until the only light remaining was that coming from the stars. At times Holley couldn't see the road and was forced to rely entirely on his horse. A couple of times he heard shouts behind.

The moon came up, big and yellow, in the east. Once when the road crested a long rise and silhouetted him against the rising moon, Holley heard a volley of reports behind. The distance was still apparently too great.

Holley's horse was now running hard, a gait he could not indefinitely maintain. Not an experienced horseman by any means, Holley could still realize the danger of traveling at this speed. The moon illuminated only stretches of the
109

road. Where it was in shadow it was treacherous even for a horse, whose vision was much better than a man's.

Twice more in the next hour, his pursuers fired at him. Once a bullet clanged against a rock immediately beside his horse and made the animal shy violently. He crested the summit of the pass and descended toward the flat reaches of South Park, called Bayou Salade by the trappers and the Indians.

His horse slowed to a trot and could not be urged to greater speed. Holley jacked a cartridge into the rifle and swung around in his saddle to study the road behind. He listened intently, but he could hear no running hoofbeats on the road. Apparently, then, the horses of the pursuit had also been forced to slow their gait.

The night air here near the top of the pass was cold. Sometimes he could hear water running at the side of the road. Wolves howled on a nearby hill, and once a cougar screamed. When that happened, Holley's horse again broke into a lope.

The lights of Fairplay were a welcome sight ahead. Holley rode immediately to the hotel, a two-story building built of stone. He tied his horse, entered and inquired about Ferguson.

The desk clerk, an elderly woman, said she hadn't seen Ferguson for several months.

Holley returned to the door and stared into the street. His gray horse was tied to the rail in front of the hotel. He realized uneasily that the Custis brothers and Kellison were either already in town, watching his tethered horse, or would arrive before he could go out and find the post office.

He went back to the hotel desk. "Is there a rear door?"

The woman frowned suspiciously at him. Grudgingly she nodded toward a door beyond the desk. "If it's the law after you . . ."

"It isn't." Holley went through the door, hurried down a long corridor and through a kitchen where a man with a white apron sat smoking a pipe. He continued out the back door into the alley, which was so dark he couldn't see a thing. He could see the ends of the alley, however, since

110

there was a little light in the two cross streets. He stood completely still long enough to be sure no one was in the alley with him. Then, hurrying, he crossed, went between two buildings and out onto the street beyond.

It could hardly be called a street, being only a two-track, muddy road. Now all he had to do, Holley thought, was to find the post office. Once the letter had been mailed he could get a room at the hotel and go to sleep. He couldn't remember ever having been so tired.

Without showing himself, he worked his way back to the main street. A stagecoach was rolling into town, throwing up huge gobs of mud from its wheels. It pulled up in front of the stage station a block down the street from the hotel. Holley watched the passengers alight.

There was a woman who looked as if she worked in a saloon. There was a man who was obviously a salesman. There were two miners and no other passengers. Ferguson still had not arrived.

Holley studied the street carefully before he moved. He guessed that the post office was probably either in or near the stage depot.

He reached it without seeing any of the Custis brothers or Kellison. There were, however, five horses tied together in front of the Pink Lady Saloon across the street from the hotel.

He ducked into the stage depot hastily, and was gratified to see a brass grille on the far side of the room with a sign hanging above it, "Post Office."

He removed the judge's letter from his pocket, crossed the room and handed it to the man behind the grille. "Will this go out tonight?"

"Not tonight. Tomorrow at four o'clock."

"Morning or afternoon?"

"Morning."

Holley gave him the letter and paid for the stamp, which the postmaster stuck on the envelope. Holley turned and went out into the street.

He returned to the hotel by the same route he had used coming from it. He entered the back door and continued through to the lobby. He went out the front door, untied his

111

horse and rode him to the livery stable at the lower end of town. The five horses were no longer tied in front of the saloon.

Having stabled his horse, Holley walked back up the street to the hotel. He went in and climbed the stairs wearily to his room. He lay down fully clothed, the rifle lying on the bed beside him.

A commotion in the street awakened him. He went to the window and peered outside. There was a cluster of men down in front of the stage depot. Some had lanterns. All were talking excitedly.

Holley went out into the hall, the rifle in his hand. He closed his door but didn't bother locking it. He hurried down the stairs and out into the street. When he reached the group in front of the stage depot the sky in the east was turning gray. He judged it was getting close to four o'clock, which was the time the Denver stage would leave.

Turning to the man next to him, he asked, "What's the commotion about?"

"Somebody robbed the post office."

Holley pushed his way into the stage depot. There were two men with stars on their vests in front of the post office grille. They were talking to the postmaster.

The room was filled with men. Holley pushed his way to the grille. It was possible there was no connection between the robbery and the fact that the Custis brothers and Kellison were in town. He overheard one of the lawmen ask, "What was taken besides money, Sam?"

"Nothin' that I can see. The mail sack for Denver was dumped out on the floor and scattered but it don't look like anything's missing from it."

Holley crowded close to the grille. "How about my letter? Is it still there? It's addressed to the U. S. marshal in Denver, Mr. Ferguson. The sender is Judge Myer in Wild Horse."

The postmaster glanced at him curiously but he dumped the sack out on the table and began to look through it. He finished and glanced up. "It ain't here."

"I didn't think it would be." Holley knew he had to get

112

back to Wild Horse. He had to get back immediately. The judge was in mortal danger. The Custis brothers would kill him if they could to prevent him from sending another letter to Ferguson.

He said, "I've got to write another letter. Can you give me paper and a pencil? And can you hold the stage until I've finished it?"

One of the lawmen started to question him but Holley said, "I'll tell you everything I know just as soon as I get this letter on the stage."

He finished writing. He addressed the envelope to the Territorial Governor, Denver. He handed it to the postmaster, who affixed a stamp and put it into the sack. The stage driver took the sack and carried it outside.

Holley swiftly told the town marshal what was going on down in Wild Horse. He told them he thought both Sheriff Mexico and Judge Myer were in danger of being killed.

Leaving, he ran to the livery barn. He saddled his own horse and rode out into the lightening gray of dawn. Kicking the horse's sides, he pointed him west toward Trout Creek Pass.

CHAPTER 18

Holley had no way of knowing how much of a start the Custis brothers and Kellison had. He had not inquired about the time of the post office robbery. He could only hope the five were not too far ahead.

The clouds in the east turned pink, then gold, and at last the sun came up. Holley drummed on the gray's sides with his heels and the horse responded willingly. He pounded across the park toward the pass that threaded through the mountains to the west.

Dew lay heavily on the grass. Holley wondered how long it would take the governor to act. He had requested troops in the sheriff's name. He had urged that the governor dispatch all federal marshals and deputies available, mentioning the post office robbery he believed committed by the five. He hoped his language would convey the urgency of the situation.

He reached the top of the pass and began the descent. Now, where the road was damp, he was able to make out the prints of the five horses traveling ahead of him. He was not, however, able to estimate how old they were.

Nervously he tried to guess what the Custis brothers and Kellison would do when they reached Wild Horse. They had Judge Myer's letter in their possession and they knew he had tried to summon help. As contemptuous of law as they were, it was conceivable they would actually harm the judge.

The sun climbed across the sky. Holley's horse seemed to travel with maddening slowness but he knew it was only his own sense of frustrated urgency. He reached the Arkansas and turned south toward the town of Wild Horse.

The last two miles, he forced the gray to run. And he was rewarded by seeing the Custis brothers enter town less than a mile ahead of him.

Court was in session at the courthouse. The judge was probably trying some civil case, Holley thought. There were a few horses tied to the rail, and there were a couple of buggies. The five horses Holley was following had gone on.

Holley heaved a sigh of relief when he saw them tied in front of the Wild Horse Saloon. He passed the saloon without looking directly at it. A spot in the middle of his back began to ache in expectation of a bullet striking it, but he reached the jail without being fired upon. He dismounted, tied the gray and went inside.

The sheriff was standing at the window watching the saloon across the street. He had a rifle in his hands and Holley knew that if any of the Custis brothers had shot at

114

him, the sheriff would have returned the fire instantly. Mexico looked at him questioningly.

Holley said, "I got to Fairplay all right, although they shot at me a couple of times along the road. I slipped out the back door of the hotel and went to the post office and mailed the judge's letter. The trouble was, they robbed the post office later and took the money and the judge's letter. So I wrote another letter, this time to the governor, and saw that it got on the stage. Then I came back. I thought they might try to kill the judge."

"They might, too, if they get liquored up. I think we ought to get him and bring him back to the jail."

Holley nodded agreement. He checked the loads in his rifle. He followed Burt Mexico out the door.

He couldn't help glancing nervously at the Wild Horse Saloon across the street because he didn't really believe they were going to let him and the sheriff go safely past. He held the rifle across his chest in a ready position, and his finger was tight on the trigger, his thumb on the hammer ready to draw it back.

The shot came from inside the saloon and was fired through the door. There was no way either he or Mexico could have seen the shooter, no way either of them could have defended himself.

Holley swung around the instant the report reached his ears. He could now see smoke billowing from above and below the swinging doors. Levering the gun rapidly, he put three shots into the doors before he turned to see if the sheriff was all right.

Mexico was down on his knees. One hand clutched his right side. Blood leaked through his fingers and dripped into the dust. His face was a ghastly shade of gray. He grunted angrily, "The dirty sons-of-bitches, they never gave us a chance!"

Holley knew the five in the saloon could now kill both of them with impunity. He didn't know why they hadn't already done so. The only reason he could think of was that perhaps even the lawless five were shocked by what one of them had done.

He said, "Let's get back in the jail before they finish us
115

off." He helped the sheriff to his feet, supporting him by pulling one of the sheriff's arms around his neck. Together they staggered toward the jail.

Holley leaned the rifle against the wall so that he could open the door. He helped Mexico inside and across the room to the office couch. He laid him down and returned quickly to recover his rifle and close the door.

Across the street two rifles boomed and the bullets showered Holley with dust from the stone wall of the jail. He snatched his rifle and ducked back inside, slamming the office door and bolting it.

He crossed the room to the sheriff's side. Mexico's face was still bloodless, his eyes narrowed with pain. Holley unbuttoned his shirt and underwear and pulled them away from the wound. Blood was pouring from it and had already soaked the couch beneath.

Holley said, "You've got to have the doc and you've got to have him quick."

"I don't know how the hell you're going to manage that. This place doesn't have a door in back."

"I'll manage it. Do you think you can stay conscious while I'm gone?"

Mexico said grimly, "I'd better, hadn't I?"

Holley went to the gun rack and took a shotgun down. He loaded it, returned and handed it to Mexico. Mexico trained the muzzle on the door. He said between his teeth, "Just let the bastards come in that door. That's all I ask."

Holley said, "I'll be right back."

He went to the window first and peered across at the saloon. He could see a rifle muzzle resting on the top of one of the swinging doors. If he got out of here without being hit, it would be a miracle. But he couldn't remain. If he did, Burt Mexico would die.

He flung open the door and plunged through it. He sprinted toward the corner of the building. Across the street, two rifles roared, and at least two revolvers echoed them. Bullets slammed into the walls of the jail. One tore through the door and another shattered a window.

Clutching his rifle, Holley reached the corner of the jail and ducked behind it. He ran toward the alley and whirled

116

into it, heading uptown toward Hiram Rounds' office next to the hotel.

When he reached the stairway leading up to it, he glanced back toward the Wild Horse Saloon.

Apparently they were still watching the jail. They hadn't guessed where he had gone. He took the stairs two at a time and burst into the doctor's office.

Rounds was standing at the window looking down into the street. He glanced at Holley.

Holley said, "Burt Mexico's been hit. It's bad and he needs you right away."

"How . . . ?"

Holley said, "Hell, I don't know how we're going to get back in. But we've got to try."

Rounds was plainly scared but he picked up his bag and put on his hat. He followed Holley down the stairs. They returned along the alley and Holley led the way through the weeds to the side of the jail. He said, "The door's unlocked. I only know of one way for you to get in. I'll blast away at them and when I yell for you to go, get in the jail door as fast as you can."

He poked his head around the corner of the jail and stared across at the Wild Horse Saloon, startled to see that the five horses were gone. Frowning, he stepped into the open, his rifle ready, his gaze on the doorway of the saloon across the street.

Nothing moved and no shots greeted him. He turned his head. "Come on, Doc. They're gone."

Doc Rounds scurried into the jail and slammed the door behind him. Holley stared up the street toward the courthouse. At this distance he couldn't be sure, but he thought he saw a couple of the horses belonging to the Custis brothers there.

He should have expected it, he supposed. They had shot the sheriff and for all they knew, Mexico could be dead. They had seen Holley leave and had probably assumed he was running away. Now they were at the courthouse and there could be only one reason for their presence there. They meant to kill the judge.

Holley's gray horse was still tied in front of the jail. He

117

had been out of the line between jail and saloon and so had escaped being hit. Holley untied him and swung to his back. He drummed with his heels and the horse loped away toward the upper end of town.

No one was on the street, but Holley could see people in the windows and doors of the store buildings on both sides of it. He could see them peering from behind curtains in the houses at its upper end. He knew it was foolish to ride openly toward the courthouse but he also knew he had no time to waste. How he was going to stop the five men from whatever they had decided to do, he had no idea. He only knew he had to try.

From the outside, the courthouse appeared to be drowsing peacefully. Holley could hear the drone of voices from inside. He slid from his horse, not taking time to tie the reins. He ran toward the courthouse door.

Just outside it, he remembered that he had not reloaded after the exchange of shots at the jail. He took a moment to remedy that oversight, then opened the door and stepped inside, ready to plunge to one side, ready to fire instantly.

Judge Myer was standing behind the bench. Ben and Lance Custis, and Kellison, were standing in the middle aisle. Ralph was on the right, Mark on the left. All had guns in their hands.

The people in the courtroom were terrified. A woman was sobbing uncontrollably. A child was screaming and no one tried to quiet him. Judge Myer shouted angrily, "I order the five of you to leave this courtroom immediately! If you do not, I shall personally see to it that you all spend the next twenty years of your lives in prison!"

Ben Custis raised his rifle deliberately. Holley guessed that he meant to shoot the judge, and brought his own gun up. Before he could line the sights on Ben, the rifle in Ben's hands billowed smoke.

The sound of the rifle, fired in this confined space, was deafening. A cloud of bluish powdersmoke rolled down the aisle all the way to the judge's bench.

But Judge Myer no longer stood behind it. He had fallen forward, his arms outstretched and clawing, as though he was trying to hold himself erect.

118

Slowly, slowly he slid back down off the bench. The sound he made as he struck the floor was in its way as shocking as the rifle shot had been. Turning to escape, Lance Curtis saw Holley at the door and yelled, "Hey! There's that goddam sodbuster, Ben!"

Lance fired as he spoke but the bullet, hastily aimed, missed and tore a hole in the door a foot from Holley's head. Holley, whose gun was aimed at Kellison, fired, and he saw Kellison go to his knees. He yanked the door open and plunged outside. Bullets ripped into the door and showered him with splinters, some of which stung his skin.

He knew there was no time to reach his horse. He knew he didn't dare stay in the open or they'd bring him down like a fleeing deer. His only hope lay in getting out of sight immediately and in reaching the jail before they could, a near impossibility considering that they would be mounted and he would be afoot.

He plunged for the corner of the courthouse building and disappeared behind it. Running hard, he reached the alley, turned into it and ran as he had never run before.

Maybe they'd be cautious about coming out, he thought. Maybe they'd figure he was waiting outside for them. He could only hope.

His breath was coming in short gasps, but he was nearly there. He whirled into the lot beside the jail and sprinted for the street. Reaching it, he plunged out into it recklessly and turned toward the jail door.

The four Custis brothers were less than a hundred yards away, coming on at a hard gallop down the middle of the street. Holley heard the roar of their guns as they opened fire on him. He saw the bullets strike the dusty street, heard them ricochet from the stone walls of the jail, heard the tinkle of glass as another window was shattered by the fusillade. He yanked open the door and flung himself inside, miraculously untouched.

Doc Rounds slammed and bolted the door. Panting hard, Holley whirled and poked his gun muzzle out a window. He fired almost instantly and saw Lance's horse go down. He fired again at Lance's running form, and saw Lance go to his knees.

119

Ben reined his horse around, giving protection to Lance, who was scrambling on all fours toward the saloon doors across the street. Holley fired at Ben and missed. Ben's great, roaring voice filled the street. "Take cover, damn it! Take cover!"

Ralph and Mark were galloping away, one up the street, one down. Ben was heading for the saloon doors, still mounted, still trying to provide protection for the wounded Lance. Turning in his saddle, he fired at Holley in the jail.

Holley fired back and he saw that Ben was hit. The man's rifle clattered to the ground and he clutched his right shoulder with his left hand. He literally fell off his horse at the saloon door, got up and ran inside. Lance had already disappeared.

Two of them were wounded and Kellison was apparently dead, thought Holley. He didn't know about Lance, but he knew Ben would be like a wounded grizzly bear, more dangerous wounded than he had ever been untouched.

CHAPTER 19

Behind him, Holley could hear the doctor talking to Burt Mexico. Mexico asked weakly, "How about it, Doc? What kind of a chance have I got?"

"None if you don't shut up and lie still."

Holley turned his head. Mexico lay on his back, his shirt open, his chest exposed. Rounds was holding a compress to the wound. "Bullet went on through," he said. "But God knows . . ."

From across the street, the Custis brothers opened up. Judging from the number of reports, Holley guessed both

120

Mark and Ralph had reached the saloon, probably by the alley door. He ducked his head, seeing no point in trading shots with them. The stone walls of the jail would stop their bullets and as long as a man didn't get in front of the windows or the door he should be safe from them.

Suddenly he cocked his head, listening. He had caught the sounds of other shots, coming from farther up the street. Frowning puzzledly, he sidled close to one of the windows and peered along the street.

The shots were coming from the windows and doors of the shops along Shavano Street. They were coming from roofs and from the upstairs windows of the hotel. One after another of the saloon windows shattered, the glass cascading noisily to the walk. Holley turned his head and grinned at Mexico. "Well! Looks like the citizens have finally got their bellies full of the Custis brothers! They're shooting at the saloon!"

Doc Rounds turned his head. "He can't hear you. He's unconscious."

"Is he going to make it?"

"I don't know. He's tough. But he's lost a lot of blood."

Holley saw the four Custis brothers break from the saloon. They opened fire on the townspeople who were shooting at them from windows and doors along Shavano Street. Ben's face was twisted. His teeth were bared with pain.

Lance went down first. Already wounded and forced to shoot from a kneeling position, he suddenly stiffened and dropped his gun. He turned his head and looked at Ben, obviously trying to say something. Then he folded forward and lay still. Ben knelt at his side, oblivious of the bullets slamming into the saloon walls in back of him.

Mark was the second of the brothers to be hit. He was driven backward to crash into Ben and Lance and collapse on top of them. Ben took one look at the wound in Mark's chest, then straightened, roaring, "Ralph! Come on!"

The two ran to their horses, untied them and swung astride. As they whirled into the street, their mounts rearing with terror and surprise, one of the other horses at the rail was hit. He tore loose and galloped up the street, to

121

fall, somersaulting, before he had gone fifty yards.

Both Ben and Ralph disappeared downstreet in a cloud of dust. Holley said, "Doc, take care of Burt. I'm going after them!" He slammed out of the jail and mounted one of the Custis brothers' horses running loose in the street.

Someone up the street yelled, "Wait, Mr. Holley! We'll go with you!" but he didn't turn his head and he didn't stop. Ben Custis was hurt and had seen Kellison and two of his brothers killed. He wasn't fleeing to be safe; he was fleeing because there was still one insane thing he had to do. He had set out to rid the country of homesteaders and he meant to do just that before he died. He was heading for Gerda Nordlander's place, knowing Holley would follow him. He was betting it would take a while before the townspeople got a posse up. In that interval he hoped to burn Gerda out and kill Holley when he came to try to put a stop to it.

The horse was willing but he was tired. Holley drummed savagely on his sides with his heels. He whipped him relentlessly with the ends of the reins. The horse began to gallop.

Holley whirled out of town and took the Shavano Creek road. He could now see Ben and Ralph ahead of him by about a quarter of a mile. Their horses were running hard, drawing slowly and relentlessly away.

Holley slammed his rifle barrel down on his horse's rump and the animal gave forth an extra burst of speed. Holley leaned low over his withers, reins in one hand, rifle in the other. He was keeping pace with Ben Custis and Ralph now, neither gaining nor losing ground. He knew that was as much as he could expect. At least he would arrive only a minute or two behind the pair. They couldn't do much damage in that length of time. They'd barely have time to set themselves.

Sweat flecked the horse's neck and sides. His breathing was harsh and rasping. Holley was aware he might kill the animal but there was nothing else that he could do. He didn't dare let Ben and Ralph draw ahead any more. If he did, he might find Gerda and her children dead when he arrived.

The horse stumbled as Holley whirled him into the Nordlander lane. He went to his knees, somersaulted and threw Holley fifty feet ahead of him. Holley let himself roll. His head struck a rock at the side of the road.

Stunned, dusty and bleeding, he lay still for a minute or two. When he stirred, it was to rise up groggily, to stare around uncomprehendingly several moments before he understood where he was.

Remembering, he snatched up his rifle and sprinted for the house. The horse, apparently unhurt by the fall, now stood with his head hanging listlessly, his sides heaving.

Holley was still a hundred yards from the house when Ben opened up on him. Rifle bullets kicked up dust at his feet, behind him and to the right and left.

Something slammed into his leg, feeling like the blow of a club. For an instant there was no pain, but his leg gave way and dumped him to the ground.

Again he rolled in the dust, carried forward by his own momentum. He rolled into the shallow ditch at the side of the narrow lane. He had clung to the rifle and now he levered a cartridge into the chamber and fired at Ben in the doorway of the barn.

Smoke curled from that door, and smoke was rising from the rear wall of the house. Ralph came into view, sprinting from the back of the house toward the open door of the barn. Holley aimed carefully, following Ralph with his gun muzzle, leading him just a little the way he had learned to lead a duck.

He fired, squeezing his shot off carefully, and was gratified to see Ralph stumble and fall flat on his face. Apparently the wound was not a fatal one because Ralph almost immediately began to crawl.

Ben laid a veritable fusillade down in the direction of Holley's hiding place and Holley was forced temporarily to duck his head. His leg was burning now where he had been hit. Looking down, he saw that his pants leg was soaked with blood.

His time, like Burt Mexico's, was running out. In a matter of minutes, bleeding at that rate, he would bleed to death. He raised his head and almost instantly Ben's rifle

123

boomed. A bullet gouged a furrow in the road a foot away from him.

Suddenly a shotgun roared in the window of the burning house. Buckshot rained like hail on the front wall of the barn. It kicked up spurts of dust all around the crawling form of Ralph, who now began to scream with pain. Apparently he had been hit with buckshot, Holley thought.

He aimed carefully at Ben, and fired. Ben flinched but he didn't fall. He took careful aim at Holley again and fired just as Holley ducked.

Flames were leaping ever higher in the barn. The back wall of the house had caught and was now shooting flames above the eaves. Smoke poured from all the open windows, even from the kitchen window through which Gerda had fired only moments before.

The door opened and Gerda appeared in it. Instantly Ben fired and his bullet tore a shower of splinters from the jamb beside her head. She ducked back in and slammed the door.

Holley couldn't tell whether Ben had deliberately missed or not. He couldn't believe that Ben would deliberately try to kill a woman and two little children. What seemed more likely was that Ben was keeping them pinned inside, knowing that by doing so he would force Holley to try reaching them.

The flames were roaring now. Burning wood cracked like pistol shots. The whole rear half of the house was burning. Smoke poured from the shattered kitchen window in a dense yellow cloud.

Unless Gerda and the children were down on the floor, they were already overcome, Holley thought, and he knew he could wait no more. Praying his leg would support him, he leaped to his feet.

Instantly Ben began firing. Holley ran toward the house, zig-zagging desperately as he ran.

Once his leg gave way and spilled him to the ground but he was up instantly, and running once again. It seemed impossible for him to reach the house without being hit.

In that instant, Ben's gunhammer clicked on an empty chamber. Holley glimpsed his face and saw the look of enraged frustration it wore. Ben flung the rifle from him and snatched for the revolver at his side.

Smoke drifted between the two, not completely obscuring vision but dimming it. Ben ran toward Holley, his revolver coming into line. . . .

Holley could hear Gerda and the children coughing inside the kitchen, but he knew he had to stop. Ben was too close. Ben would kill him and he would do Gerda no good if he were dead.

He halted and brought the rifle to his shoulder. He fired the split part of a second before Ben did. The two reports were so close together they were virtually indistinguishable.

Holley's bullet struck Ben just as his finger squeezed the trigger. He was driven back toward the fiercely blazing barn. His bullet stirred the hair above Holley's ear.

Holley didn't wait to see him fall. He slammed into the house, pausing an instant until he located them by the sound of their voices. He roared, "Gerda! It's all right now! Come out!"

He saw movement in the billowing yellowish cloud of smoke and then he was lifting her, and helping the children out. His eyes were streaming and he was coughing uncontrollably just as Gerda and the children were.

Outside, he pulled them far enough away from the house to get out of the smoke and heat. He looked toward the barn and saw Ben lying motionless on his back. Ralph lay unconscious nearby, his chest rising and falling regularly.

Weakness overcame Holley now. His head whirled and he felt himself falling. Gerda tried to catch him but he pulled her down with him as he fell.

Her hair was singed and her face smudged but he thought he had never seen anything more beautiful. She was tearing cloth from her skirt and making a compress for his wound and holding it tightly there while she bound it in place with strips of cloth. The children lay still and listless on the ground, gasping gratefully at the clear, pure air.

And now the people from town came riding into the yard. They formed a bucket brigade to try to put the fires out but it was too late to save anything. They gave up at last, and hitched up the buckboard and loaded Holley and

125

Gerda and the children into it. They loaded Ralph and Ben's body into another rig and started back to town.

Holley lay with his head in Gerda's lap. His farm in Illinois seemed very far away.

He had hated this land for killing Jed and he had hated it for its lawlessness, and for its violence.

But the violence was over now and he knew his future lay right here. Other homesteaders would come to claim the land and they would be safe because the people of the community would make them safe.

It didn't seem to matter anymore who had killed Jed. Indifference on the part of the community had been the real murderer. Now that indifference was gone.

Lewis B. Patten wrote more than ninety Western novels in thirty years and three of them won Spur Awards from the Western Writers of America and the author himself the Golden Saddleman Award. Indeed, this highlights the most remarkable aspect of his work: not that there is so much of it, but that so much of it is so fine. Patten was born in Denver, Colorado, and served in the U.S. Navy 1933–1937. He was educated at the University of Denver during the war years and became an auditor for the Colorado Department of Revenue during the 1940s. It was in this period that he began contributing significantly to Western pulp magazines, fiction that was from the beginning fresh and unique and revealed Patten's lifelong concern with the sociological and psychological affects of group psychology on the frontier. He became a professional writer at the time of his first novel, *Massacre at White River* (1952). The dominant theme in much of his fiction is the notion of justice, and its opposite, injustice. In his first novel it has to do with exploitation of the Ute Indians, but as he matured as a writer he explored this theme with significant and poignant detail in small towns throughout the early West. Crimes, such as rape or lynching, were often at the centre of his stories. When the values embodied in these small towns are examined closely, they are found to be wanting. Conformity is always easier than taking a stand. Yet, in Patten's view of the American West, there is usually a man or a woman who refuses to conform. Among his finest titles, always a difficult choice, surely are *A Killing at Kiowa* (1972), *Ride a Crooked Trail* (1976), and his many fine contributions to Doubleday's Double D series, including *Villa's Rifles* (1977), *The Law at Cottonwood* (1978), and *Death Rides a Black Horse* (1978). His most recent books are *Tincup in the Storm Country* (1996), *Trail to Vicksburg* (1997), *Death Rides the Denver Stage* (1999), and *The Woman at Ox-Yoke* (2000).